I0676863

Mistletoe Magic

by

Annette Miller

This is a work of fiction. Names, characters, places, and incidents are either the product of the author's imagination or are used fictitiously, and any resemblance to actual persons living or dead, business establishments, events, or locales, is entirely coincidental.

Mistletoe Magic

COPYRIGHT © 2023 by Annette Miller

All rights reserved. No part of this book may be used or reproduced in any manner whatsoever without written permission of the author or The Wild Rose Press, Inc. except in the case of brief quotations embodied in critical articles or reviews.
Contact Information: info@thewildrosepress.com

Cover Art by *Kristian Norris*

The Wild Rose Press, Inc.
PO Box 708
Adams Basin, NY 14410-0708
Visit us at www.thewildrosepress.com

Publishing History
First Edition, 2023
Trade Paperback ISBN 978-1-5092-5162-9
Digital ISBN 978-1-5092-5201-5

Published in the United States of America

"I'm sorry." Mel dusted her hands off on her jeans. "How can I help you?"

"I'm Conner Andrews from Andrews Travel. I'm supposed to meet with Dee Warner and Melissa Owens?"

Mel's mouth went dry as she tried to tighten her loose ponytail and straighten her clothes. "I'm Melissa," she said, as she brushed off more dust from her sweater. "Everyone calls me Mel. Have you talked to Aunt Dee yet?"

"Yes. I met her and your sister Alexandra. Mrs. Warner said she didn't want to discuss any plans until you were present. She said you have more of the information I requested."

"I'll tell you all I can. What do you think of the B and B so far?" she asked, as she tried to keep the tremor from her voice. "Do you think you'd be interested in adding it to your company's listings?"

"From what I've seen, this place is very…quaint. I don't want to say any more until we have a chance to sit down and talk."

Mel watched Conner walk away. He'd called their B and B quaint. Why did it sound like he didn't find it quite as appealing as the word "quaint" would have her believe?

Praise

"[NIGHT ANGEL] is the first book in Ms. Miller's Angel Haven series, and I'm hoping she will come up with a bunch more." ~Annetta Sweetco, Fresh Fiction Reviews~

An Angel's Heart finaled in the American Fiction Awards Paranormal Romance Category in 2018

Angel in Shadow finaled in the American Fiction Awards Paranormal Romance Category in 2020

Praline Dreams won 1st Place in the International Digital Awards Short Paranormal Category in 2020

Macaroons by Moonlight won 1st Place in the Heart Awards Short Paranormal Category in 2021 and finaled in the Golden Leaf Awards in 2022

Dedication

For my husband Brian, and my sons, Scot and Alex.
You guys made me believe I could achieve my dream.

Prologue

The pale blue door in the corner of Delia Warner's small office creaked open. Ivory curtains billowed for a moment then settled back as Melissa and Alexandra Owens stepped through in a flurry of snowflakes. They shook the snow out of their hair and brushed off their coats. They made sure to wipe most of the moisture from the bottom of their heavy boots before they walked in any farther.

The office hadn't changed in all the years since Delia Warner had opened her bed and breakfast. She'd converted the smallest room on the ground floor of the three-story Victorian home as her personal office. The sisters always loved to come visit their aunt, more so at Christmas. This time of year, Delia would go all out with decorations at the B and B for her guests. If she wasn't here in her office, she could be found in her kitchen as she made the most wonderful meals and desserts.

Melissa didn't see anyone, only a mound of paper on the desk by the door. Silence surrounded them as they stepped farther in. The sisters looked at each other. Aunt Dee could be in the kitchen, or had gone through the green door to visit Mrs. C. They walked over to the door which led to the lobby of the B and B.

"Aunt Dee," Melissa called out, as she looked around for her aunt. "We got your message. We're here to help."

Dee Warner rushed to the office and stepped inside. The short, older lady with sparkling blue eyes and silver hair hurried over and hugged her nieces. The bright red poinsettia tucked into her hair matched the red shirt she wore under a white vest. Forest green pants completed her holiday outfit.

"I'm so glad the two of you were able to come," Dee said. "I don't know what I would have done if you couldn't make it. Now, before we get to the matter at hand, how is the winter kingdom these days? Do you have any news from my sister?"

"About the same as always, covered in snow. And you know what they say about no news. It might be good news," Mel said, as she and her sister hung up their coats. "Mom told us Garland Falls has some kind of problem. Can you give us a clue?"

"The fresh mistletoe hasn't arrived yet." Dee wrung her hands, and a worried frown creased her brows. "Christmas is right around the corner, and the magic has started to fade. Some of the doorways to the other kingdoms don't open like they should. Thank goodness the door to the winter kingdom still works or you two wouldn't have been able to come. We're all very concerned. I'm afraid of what will happen if we don't get new mistletoe soon."

"Does the green door to the North Pole still work?" Alex asked. "If not, we'd have a major problem to worry about. How can we get the children's letters delivered if we can't open the portal?"

"The North Pole door hasn't had any problems so far," Dee said. "I think it's because of the power of the holiday spirit. I fear it's a matter of time, though."

Mel and Alex looked at each other. For Aunt Dee to ask for help from the winter kingdom with Christmas so close told them the situation was worse than she let on. The spritely woman could handle any crisis with plenty of optimism and not the worry she showed now.

"I've sent a letter to the Andrews Travel Agency," Dee continued. "If we can get a representative up here, maybe he'll be able to add Warner's Bed and Breakfast and Garland Falls to their travel listings."

"You contacted a human company?" Mel said.

"Are you sure you've made the right decision? This little town doesn't have a whole lot to offer to tourists," Alex said. "And we all know how Garland Falls feels about strangers."

"If it's good for the town, the people and the town should be okay with it, right?" Mel laid her hand on her sister's shoulder. "And maybe Aunt Dee is right. It wouldn't hurt to try to attract more business to the B and B and the town. I've heard a new business opened here last fall."

"And it's been a great addition to Main Street," Dee said. "Our festivals draw in the crowds, but this year, every store in town is down in sales. I haven't had as many reservations for the upcoming winter carnival." She tapped her chin, and her mischievous smile came out. "I contacted Andrews Travel because I believe they have a connection to Garland Falls."

"Do you know these people? If so, you've never mentioned them." Mel said. She narrowed her eyes. "What aren't you telling us, Aunt Dee?"

"I know the family name. I want to see if my instincts still work like they should. As the humans like to say, I've decided to play a hunch."

"Hunches can be very wrong sometimes," Alex said. "Do we know who's coming here yet?"

"Not yet," Dee said.

"You know Aunt Dee will tell us when she wants to." Mel looked at her sister, who shrugged. "We're here now and we'll do what we can to help. Alex has learned to bake and she's pretty good at it. She took lessons from Mrs. C."

"Should we have a booth at the carnival?" Alex said. "I'd be more than happy to help prepare baked goods."

"I'll consider it," Dee said. She walked over to her office chair and sat. "By this time in the month, I'm too busy here to have a booth, but not this year." She waved at the stack of paper on her desk. "And the bills have started to pile up. Booth sales would help boost the bank account more."

"Did Andrews Travel give us a definite for someone to come? I mean, you did get a reply, right? Any advice they can offer will be a big help," Mel said.

"I have indeed heard back from them." Dee picked up a letter and stared at it. "Someone should be here next week. We don't have much time to get this place in tiptop shape." She sighed. "If the mistletoe would come, I know we'd be fine."

"Well, until it does, Alex and I will have to be enough." Her sister nodded at Mel's statement. "The mistletoe will be here before you know it. Garland Falls always survives and it will this time, too."

"I hope you're right, dear." Dee turned to look out the window. Snow had begun to fall, and the front driveway glittered in the sunset's fading light. "I hope you're right."

Chapter One

Why did he ever listen to his mother? And why couldn't she give him the same courtesy.

Conner Andrews threw the last of his socks into the suitcase as his mother walked into his room. He refused to turn around to see the disappointed look in her eyes. He grabbed a few more shirts from the closet, folded them, and pressed them into the bag.

"And now you refuse to talk to me?" she asked. "You know you and Felicia Hawthorn were meant for each other. You need to marry the girl and be done with it. I don't approve of this spur of the moment trip. Your place is here."

He turned as he raked a hand through his hair. "Marriage should be more than a recommendation from a parent, Mom. Felicia and I will get married when the time is right for us and not before. I have to get up north to Garland Falls, Minnesota to check out the B and B the owner wrote us about. I'll call you when I arrive."

His mother shuddered and folded her arms. "I don't understand why you have to go to this obscure town. I've been there, and believe me, it doesn't bear to be investigated. I told Michael he needed to be the one who should go, but the two of you fought me tooth and toenail. You need to stay and plan your wedding."

"There won't be a wedding." He picked up the suitcase and walked toward her. "At least not for some time. Felicia and I want to make sure we're ready."

He stared at his mother. Even in her early sixties, Katherine Andrews still had the classic beauty of her youth. Of course, he felt certain the plastic surgery and blonde hair dye played more than a small part. They lived in the more upscale neighborhood outside Coco Beach in Florida. She always insisted a certain image be maintained at all times. Conner had let his light brown hair grow out to what she considered an unkempt length. She called him spiteful, but he wanted to be his own person.

"But to go all the way to Minnesota at this time of year? It will be cold with snow everywhere." She folded her arms and glared at him. "I know you've always wanted to go to Garland Falls because your father used to live there. However, I doubt this insignificant B and B is worth all this trouble to add to our travel agency. Can they even afford to be listed with us? We're a very exclusive company with a price range I don't believe this place can afford. I don't think our clients will be interested."

"You never know how tastes will change. I have to admit, I became interested when we got the offer to see the B and B. Besides, I'd like to see where Dad grew up." He gave her a quick peck on the cheek. "He always talked about Garland Falls, so I want to make the trip. I need to see firsthand what they have to offer and what the town is like."

"But, Conner, this is our busy season. Christmas is right around the corner, and you're expected at the events I've planned," she shouted. "Michael will need your help, more than ever."

"Michael can handle any and all situations. Our

office manager works well with him. He'll have all the help he needs while I'm away." He kissed her cheek one more time. "Besides, Dad always said any new travel spot is worth the time spent to get there. My side of the business is to go to new places, so I'm going."

"But, Conner…"

He walked down the wide, oak staircase and crossed the marble tiled floor to the front door. Each staccato tap of his mother's heels behind him made him flinch. "Don't worry, Mom. I should be back by Christmas."

He walked out to his SUV, tossed his suitcase in the trunk, and got into the driver's seat. He watched his mother stand on the porch, her arms folded, as her foot tapped out a quick rhythm. He knew that stance all too well. Her anger radiated out toward him because he'd defied her wishes. He expected to get a few angry phone calls from her while he checked out Garland Falls.

He waved and pulled out. He needed this time away from the parties and social elite in Florida. He hoped, in his absence, Felicia and his brother might get their chance to be alone. They were the ones who were meant to be together. He and Felicia would never be more than good friends. Katherine had to be the only one who couldn't see or understand Michael's and Felicia's relationship as it blossomed right under her nose. He hoped it would become clear to her in his absence.

He hummed along to the radio and merged onto the interstate. He headed north to what could turn out to be a great location. Bags rustled in the back seat. He had ordered plenty of winter gear for the northern weather.

On the passenger seat, a tiny sprig of mistletoe vibrated in time to the hum of the tires on the road. He glanced at it and wondered why Dee Warner had sent it in her letter to him. Even stranger, he couldn't bring himself to throw it away.

****

Conner's mother stomped as hard as she could in her designer heels back into the house. Her eldest son would drive her to an early grave with his attitude. She paused before a picture of Conner and Michael. The brothers were similar in appearance, but Conner favored her late husband more. He had the broad shoulders, square jaw, light brown hair, and the gray eyes of his father.

Michael's shoulders and chest weren't as wide as Conner's, but he had his brother's height. He had the same light brown hair but had inherited her blue eyes. He ran the business when Conner traveled to make contacts to build their hotel list for the family travel agency. Her gaze traveled to her husband. He smiled in the picture she picked up. He'd always had a smile for everyone but saved his special ones for her.

When he passed away, Katherine thought her heart would break. She placed the picture back on the small table and sighed. She'd been glad her boys had a knack for the business. She didn't know what she would have done if they hadn't taken over. Her skills lay in socializing with prospective clients. She planned different events so they could meet and get to know her family. The Andrews family made a good team with all their talents.

She loved both her sons, even if some outside people didn't think so. Yes, she could be hard on them at times, but it made them better men in the long run. Her husband had been the nurturer, and she'd had the hard task of disciplinarian. She'd disliked the role more and more as her sons grew into young adults. However, she'd fallen back on it when Silas had passed away. If she could keep her boys close, they'd be with her forever. As time went on, it got harder and harder to back off from the hard stance she'd taken.

She took a deep breath and walked to the small, sunlit room off the kitchen. She'd had the walls painted light yellow with a pale blue, almost white ceiling. From here she could see the gardens and catch the scent of the flowers in the spring and summer when she opened the window. Her three-shelf bookcase stood against the wall by the door, a small desk next to it. Her recliner, with a table to the right of it, sat positioned at an angle in the middle of the room.

She'd turned this room into her private spot, where she could rest and get her thoughts together. She sat in the recliner and picked up her book from the end table. She stared at it for a moment, then replaced it and glanced up when the cook came in.

"Yes?"

"Should I serve your lunch in here now, ma'am?"

Katherine nodded. "Yes, please, with lavender tea to calm me down."

As the sunshine warmed her, she frowned as she thought about Conner as he drove north. He didn't even want to fly. She wanted him to hurry back and marry Felicia before the girl decided to call off the engagement. Felicia's parents loved Conner and a marriage would help her keep them as clients for a long, long time. If her eldest son could understand the important ramifications of this marriage, her job would be much easier.

****

Conner checked the time. He'd been on the road for almost twelve hours. He groaned as the GPS showed he had at least another ten hours to go. He found a hotel off the highway and took the exit. It would upset his mother's plans if he got hurt because he didn't stop and rest. He pulled into the first hotel he found, and the mistletoe turned back toward the highway before it settled back on the seat. He frowned as he picked it up before he tucked it into his coat pocket.

He checked in and realized all the restaurants would be closed at eleven thirty at night. He grabbed a granola bar out of his bag and a bottle of water and made a plan to get up early and get breakfast. He opened his laptop and logged into the hotel's WiFi. Time to check the weather in Minnesota. After all, December was half gone. They had to get snow soon, if it hadn't fallen already.

Yep, the area around Garland Falls already had a good bit of snow on the ground and they expected more by the weekend. He'd better not linger over breakfast tomorrow so he could arrive before any more hit the ground. After he'd been to different parts of the United States and other countries, he felt confident he could drive in any precipitation that would fall from the sky, but that didn't mean he enjoyed driving while snow was falling.

He raised his bottle in a salute and said, "Thanks, Dad, for making me learn how to drive in different weather conditions by taking me all over the world.

Cheers."

Conner climbed under the covers and settled down. Tomorrow, he'd be in Garland Falls, Minnesota. It had already snowed, so he'd love to get an idea of what the town could offer with deep drifts of snow on the ground. He couldn't wait to see the B and B the owner had written to him about. He peered at the mistletoe he'd been given.

He felt, in his gut, there could be more to this tiny sprig than he knew. When he got to Garland Falls, he'd have to ask Dee Warner about it. His eyes drifted shut and his dreams were filled with dancing fairies, who all carried mistletoe in their tiny hands.

Chapter Two

Melissa knocked on the doorframe to her aunt's office. "Aunt Dee, are you okay? We heard you walking around in the middle of the night."

Dee sat back and pushed away from the desk. She tossed her glasses on top of the mound of paperwork and rubbed her eyes. "I'm fine, Mel. I couldn't sleep with so much on my mind. I hope the representative from Andrews Travel will be able to help us. We've lost a lot of reservations because of all the town's recent problems. We haven't made enough to break even this year."

Mel ran over and put her arms around her aunt's shoulders. "We'll be all right. We've always come through before."

"Yes, when we had the mistletoe delivered on time." Dee patted her arm. "If we don't get the shipment soon, there won't be any magic to protect our town. If the magic fades completely, the wards will follow."

Mel kissed the top of Dee's head. "I get it, but we won't let that happen. Hasn't Callahan's gotten the new delivery yet? He always knows how to get hard to find items."

"Not yet. Lucas said he would call me as soon as it arrives." She looked up at her niece. "Since we haven't received the fresh sprigs yet, the late delivery is the cause of our current bad luck. We haven't had a fresh batch of mistletoe since before Thanksgiving, and even his last delivery had been less than usual. I don't hold out much hope if Callahan's Floral Emporium doesn't get any more."

"We'll save the mistletoe problem for another day." Mel winked at her aunt. "Maybe the local leprechauns can help out with a bit of luck."

Dee chuckled. "It'd be nice if they did, but they're very private so and so's." She squeezed Mel's hand. "I'd like to thank you and Alex again for coming to help me through this season. I felt sure my sister needed you in the winter kingdom. The crystaling fairies might have needed help with the snow patterns and to gather the frost for the town Christmas tree."

"Not a problem, Aunt Dee. Mom said the crystalings are way ahead of schedule this year." She grinned. "At least the frost will be here on time."

Footsteps pounded through the dining room and skidded to a stop at the office door. "Mel," her sister shouted. "The kitchen sink has leaked all over the floor again. I thought you fixed it."

"I did. Let me grab my tools and I'll see what happened this time." Mel gave her aunt a final kiss and headed to the door. She stopped and looked over her shoulder. "When the fresh mistletoe arrives, make sure you hang some on the plumbing. It needs all the magic it can get."

Mel hurried to the hall closet and pulled out her toolbox. She dropped to her knees and immediately felt the cold water seeping into her pants. She opened the cabinet door and groaned out loud. The new seal she'd put on the other day had split. She reached behind the pipes and shut the water off while it splashed her face. Time for another trip to the hardware store.

Alex leaned down to get a closer look. "Do you think you can fix it one more time?"

Mel looked over her shoulder. "Yes. It's the seal again. I don't understand how the same part broke within two days though. It must have been defective. I'll talk to Lou. Maybe he's got a thicker seal I can use."

Her sister walked on tip toes over to the kitchen door. "I don't know what Aunt Dee would do without you, Mel. You've picked up quite a knack for repair work."

"Well, my dear Alexandra, let's hope we never find out. As long as someone can tell me what to do, my repair skills can only get better." Mel walked out of the kitchen, Alex right behind her. "I need to put on some dry clothes and head to the store. The representative from Andrews Travel should arrive soon. When whoever it is gets here, can you let Aunt Dee know? As you know, she needs this person to list the B and B with their agency. She hopes it will bring in a lot more business."

"You got it. Stop Niagara Falls coming out from under the sink, and I'll be happy."

"I'll do my level best," Mel said. "This time, it better stay fixed, or our pipes and I will have a long talk about constant breakage."

After changing her clothes, Mel hurried out to her aunt's small pickup truck and backed down the driveway. As she turned toward town, a new model SUV made the turn up to the B and B. She prayed the car held more people coming to check in to attend the winter carnival. They needed all the guests they could get right now. The number of visitors to the carnival had dropped off significantly this year, which meant every business in town, including Warner's Bed and Breakfast, suffered.

The bell tinkled over the door as Mel walked in. "Hey, Lou. I need another seal for the kitchen sink. The one I put on the other day split."

The older man limped around the counter, and his blues eyes twinkled with mischief. He'd combed his silver hair back and his blue flannel shirt hung over the small potbelly he sported. "I suppose Dee's blamed it on the fact she hasn't gotten the new mistletoe to refresh the magic?"

She laughed. "You know my aunt way too well. However, we've never had this many problems when the new mistletoe came on time."

Lou handed her the new seal and they walked back up to the front. "She may be right, you know. My arthritis has acted up ever since the last bundle she brought me wilted." He winked. "Don't tell her my secret."

"Cross my heart." She pulled out her wallet and handed him three ones. "Keep the change. If this happens again, I can use the credit."

"I didn't want to charge you, Mel, since I sold you a defective one last time."

"I suspect a defective part isn't the case." She leaned on the counter and sighed. "If the mistletoe would come in, I know all the problems would clear up. Either way, let me pay you. You've been a big help with all the advice on the repairs and good prices on tools."

"You know I'd do whatever I can for you and Dee. Come back and see me soon." He winked. "But a social call, not for any more repair related topics."

"Let's hope a social call will be the reason, though I don't hold out much hope," she said. "If I have to fix one more appliance, people will believe I'm from the tinker realm and not a princess of the winter kingdom."

"Very true, my girl. Very true."

Mel waved as she walked out and got in her truck. She glared at the part in her hand and frowned. "You'd better not break on me," she muttered. "If you do, you and I will have a lot of problems, understand?"

She arrived at the B and B and drove around back to the kitchen door. It wouldn't do for the guests to see her in her work clothes. She smiled as she walked in when the mop and bucket were by the sink. Alex had cleaned up before her aunt could.

She glanced at the wall clock and wondered when the person from Andrews Travel would arrive. As she crawled under the sink, she hoped to have the repair completed and could change before he'd get there. It wouldn't do for the representative to see her not at her presentable best.

Mel wiped her hands on her jeans and turned the water back on. She counted to ten as she held her breath. So far, so good. The new seal appeared to hold up. She blew out a sigh of relief. Finally, a repair had gone right, and about time, too. One problem down, about a thousand to go.

Alex poked her head in the kitchen. "Is it fixed?"

"For now. I think we may need to replace the plumbing soon. I hope the travel guy can help us make some money. We'll need it and all the magic we can summon."

"He got here as soon as you left." Alex nudged her. "He's gorgeous. He looks like your type."

"Oh, please, Alex. I don't have a type," Mel said. "I need to focus on Aunt Dee right now. There's no time for any types. Besides, once we get back to the winter kingdom, we both have to pick our consorts. Winter pixies have to pledge soon, you know. It helps to strengthen the Christmas magic."

Alex waved her hand. "Yeah, yeah, yeah. You've told me this many times since December started. Trust me about a guy for once. He's single and he's nice. Aunt Dee and I bet you'll like him. Maybe your consort is here in the mortal world, not in the winter kingdom."

Mel rolled her eyes. "Stop it, right now. Let me see how nice he is once he finds out how bad our bills are."

"Aunt Dee loves him."

"She would. Aunt Dee loves everyone." Mel double checked the faucet and nodded when the new seal still held. "Let's go avert the next disaster."

As they headed back to the lobby, Mel and Alex's ten-year-old nephew lay flat on the floor and peered under the couch in the drawing room. He had asked to stay with them until after the holidays. Bobby had dust in his dark blond hair and on the front of his T-shirt. She sighed and added one more item to her already long list of tasks.

Mel walked over and brushed off as much of the dust as she could. "What did you lose, buddy?"

"Fred." Bobby put his hands on his hips and frowned. "He got out again. Why won't he stay in his house?"

"I think I need to build a better cage for him." Mel

got down on her hands and knees and joined the search. "He knocked the lid off again, didn't he?"

"Yeah." The boy lay on his stomach as he looked under the wingback chair. "I don't want anybody to step on him."

Alex squatted next to him. "And we don't want him to scare the other guests either, do we?"

He shook his head and continued to look under furniture and behind the potted plants. Alex helped him check the rest of the drawing room as Mel went out to look behind the check-in counter. Crouched in a dark corner, sat the elusive pet.

"There you are," she murmured. "Fred, you have to stop getting out. You make Bobby sad when you do. You also hold me up from working on the repairs around here. Come here, silly boy."

She reached into the dark corner and coached a large, hairy tarantula onto her hand and sat back on her heels. "Poor baby," she said, as she stroked his brown and black fur. She rose to her feet from behind the check-in desk. "You must be scared to death."

"Not usually," said a deep voice.

Mel jumped and stumbled back until her back hit the wall. A tall man stood there, a small smile on his face. He had to be the most gorgeous man she'd ever seen. Light brown hair, gray eyes lit with humor, square jaw, broad shoulders, and taller than her by a good six inches. He wore a pullover sweater, dark blue jeans, and sturdy boots.

"I'm sorry," she squeaked out when she found her voice. "We had a runaway pet who needed to be found." She held up the large spider and he raised his eyebrows in question. "I found him."

"Fred," Bobby squealed as he ran over to her.

She deposited the tarantula in the boy's hand and smiled as he walked away. "Alex, would you go with him and put the largest book we have on the lid of the terrarium? One that will keep Fred in his home."

"Will do."

"I'm sorry." Mel dusted her hands off on her jeans. "How can I help you?"

"I'm Conner Andrews from Andrews Travel. I'm supposed to meet with Dee Warner and Melissa Owens?"

Mel's mouth went dry as she tried to tighten her loose ponytail and straighten her clothes. "I'm Melissa," she said, as she brushed off more dust from her sweater. "Everyone calls me Mel. Have you talked to Aunt Dee yet?"

"Yes. I met her and your sister Alexandra. Mrs. Warner said she didn't want to discuss any plans until you were present. She said you have more of the information I requested."

"I'll tell you all I can. What do you think of the B and B so far?" she asked, as she tried to keep the tremor from her voice. "Do you think you'd be interested in adding it to your company's listings?"

"From what I've seen, this place is very…quaint. I don't want to say any more until we have a chance to sit down and talk."

Mel watched Conner walk away. He'd called their B and B quaint. Why did it sound like he didn't find it quite as appealing as the word "quaint" would have her believe?

Chapter Three

Mel wanted to bang her head against the countertop. Conner Andrews had arrived and how did she greet him? She looked like an absolute mess with a giant tarantula on her hand. So much for a good first impression. She hoped he wouldn't hold this against her. She had to admit, though, Alex didn't lie. She'd never seen anyone so gorgeous.

"What do you think of Mr. Andrews?" her aunt said from behind her.

"I think he hates me."

Dee laughed and patted Mel's shoulder. "He doesn't hate you. You surprised him. After all, you popped up from behind the counter like a cartoon character."

"With a huge tarantula on my hand." Mel sighed. "Did he give any indication of what he thinks about the place?"

"No." Dee grinned. "He's got a great poker face."

Mel glanced at her aunt. "I hear more in your sentence than what you mean."

Dee headed back to her office, Mel right behind her. "He's very handsome," Dee said.

"I'll concede the handsome point, Aunt Dee."

Mel sprawled on the couch and watched her aunt pick up a paper from the pile which had grown overnight. "Don't even think about me and him being a couple. Like I told Alex, I don't have a type and I don't want a type. Why can't the two of you stay out of my love life?"

"If you had a love life," Dee said, as she stared at the paper in her hand, "we would. It will be hard for you when you get back home. Your mother expects you to make your choice, and the winter pixie queen is not to be denied. Now go get cleaned up. Mr. Andrews may want to do some preliminary work tonight and you look like my handyman."

"Fine." Mel pushed up from the couch. "But there's one way I'll look like your handyman and it's if I turn into Lou. He says hi, by the way. Oh, and don't forget, I am your current handyman."

"Out. Get yourself cleaned up."

Mel laughed as she made her way to her room.

****

Conner stared out his room's window. It faced the front of the house, and he had a great view of the road, the woods, and the town down the hill. There were a lot of good points to the B and B, but he'd seen some problems. It would take a lot of money to get the place up to his agency's standards.

From what he could see, Garland Falls had to be the smallest town he'd ever been in. He could see one road, and figured it had to be the main street through the center of the little town. Town? Ha, village might be a better description. Would his clients like to visit a place this small? Garland Falls didn't have a lot to offer the social elite. His thoughts returned to the lobby of the B and B.

The mahogany check-in counter made a great complement to light tan hardwood floors. A nice mahogany staircase, a pretty drawing room, a spacious dining room were all good points, but he'd noticed a draft behind him through the front door. He'd ask Dee Warner to correct it and point out it would help lower her heat bill.

The drawing room had a large Christmas tree in front of the window. Multi-colored lights twinkled off the glass ornaments and red and green garland. A lace runner with red poinsettias lay across the mantelpiece atop a big fireplace. Christmas decorations of Santas, reindeer, snowmen, and other cute statues added a comfortable holiday feel. He scratched the back of his neck. A strange sense about the B and B filled him. He couldn't put his finger on it, and it didn't set him on edge, but the sensation made him a little uncomfortable. Ever since he walked in, an annoying itch had started in his brain.

His cell phone buzzed, and he breathed a sigh of relief when he saw his brother's name. He'd dodged the "Mom bullet" for right now. "Hey, Michael. How's the situation down south?"

"Not bad, if you discount Mom's bad mood ever since you left." He chuckled. "If I'd known she'd turn into Hurricane Katherine, I would've gone with you."

"I wish you could have, but I need you in our main office." Conner stared out the window again. "This B and B has its own charm, but I'm not sure if it's right for us. It needs a lot of work."

"We've represented other properties we had brought up to what we'd like to see. What's wrong with the B and B? Is it haunted?"

Conner sat on the bed and scratched the back of his neck again. No need to mention the weird vibe crawling through his body to his brother, yet. "No, I haven't seen any ghosts, but I met this girl who works here. She held a huge tarantula in her hands."

He pulled the phone away from his ear as Michael laughed out loud. "Are you serious? We have got to take Mom up there to meet her. Besides her penchant for spiders, what's she like? Is she pretty?"

"You could call her pretty, in a country sort of way." Conner shrugged, even though he knew Michael couldn't see it. "I talked to her for a moment. I'm going to talk with her and her aunt tomorrow. Twenty-one hours in a car can wipe you out. I need to grab some dinner, then turn in. I'll call you tomorrow afternoon."

"Can't wait to hear from you. I also want to hear more about this girl you find pretty. Later."

Conner put the phone on the nightstand, laid his head against the headboard, and closed his eyes. He couldn't focus on the job, but he could picture two large, clear, ice blue eyes in a heart shaped face. Strands of honey-brown hair had escaped the sagging ponytail and she'd tried hard to fix it.

Melissa Owens, otherwise known as Mel, stood much shorter than his six-foot height with a tiny waist and small hands dwarfed by the tarantula. He'd described Mel as pretty, but he knew what she had went deeper than looks. She'd been the one to render him speechless, not the huge spider on her hand. When he looked at her, warmth had spread through him, and it tingled his nerves while his heart beat faster.

He smiled when he remembered her shocked expression when he'd introduced himself. She must have wanted to look a little nicer before she met with him. He always trusted his instincts when he met someone for the first time. Everyone he'd come in contact with in Coco Beach strutted around, all primped and polished, and only showed him their good side.

Mel, with all her untidiness while she chased a little boy's runaway pet struck him as more honest and more likeable than anyone he knew in Florida. Here, he could be free to be himself. Back home, he always had to be perfect or face his mother later for the inevitable set down. He was a grown man and still the woman had the ability to dress him down as if he were a child who misbehaved.

Conner jumped up and grabbed his coat. Time to find some dinner. He walked down the short flight of stairs and saw Alex and Mel at the check-in counter. As he headed their way, Alex excused herself and went into the office.

Mel had cleaned up and now wore jeans and a loose sweater. Her honey-brown hair had been contained in a tight ponytail. She gave him a bright, polite smile when he walked over.

"Mr. Andrews, how can I help you?"

He shrugged into his coat and zipped it up. "I wanted to find a place to eat. Can you recommend some place close with good food?"

"Yes. If you follow the road in front of the B and B, it leads into Main Street. Sal's Diner is about five minutes away and will be on the right."

"Would you care to join me?" He surprised himself with the invitation, then added, "This way you can tell me about the B and B and Garland Falls. If I list this place on our website, I need to know why people should come here."

When Mel hesitated, Conner thought she would

refuse, but then she smiled a wide, genuine smile. "Sounds like a plan. Let me grab my coat."

While he waited, he saw Dee and Alex peek out from behind the office door and look at each other. He nodded to them as he put his coat on and wondered what he'd gotten himself into.

****

Mel ran to her room and snatched her coat from the hook on the back of her door. Okay, yes. Her aunt and sister were right about his good looks. Her instant attraction to Conner Andrews caught her by surprise, and he'd asked her to have dinner with him. She took a deep breath and let it out.

"It's dinner, no more, no less," she said to her reflection in the dresser mirror. "We'll discuss business, and I won't act like a fool because he asked me to go with him. I will not consider him a candidate as my consort, though it could be nice." She forced herself to walk at a sedate pace as she headed for the lobby. "Ready when you are."

He held the door open for her, and they stepped out into the crisp, cold evening. "Shall we?" he said, as he followed her out.

Chapter Four

The diner had a large dinner crowd, and Conner started when Mel grabbed his hand. Her palm warmed his, and he wondered if she'd felt the same zing he did. She pushed past two men who looked like twins and hurried to the last empty booth. When they frowned, she laughed, the sound of it making him smile.

"Sorry, Callahans," she called out. "You snooze, you lose."

They smiled and waved as they walked to the counter. "We'll beat you next time, Mel," said the one wearing a black cowboy hat. "Count on it."

"Until then, chalk up another win for Team Owens," she said, as she drew a one in the air with her finger.

Conner laid his coat on the seat beside him. "And who are those two?"

"The one with the cowboy hat is Lucas Callahan. He owns the local nursery. Everyone in town goes to him for flowers for any occasion. The other one is his brother, Parker, who works as a groundskeeper at my aunt's B and B."

A petite, redheaded waitress hurried over to take their order and put down two glasses of water. Mel skimmed the menu and closed it. "Sally, this place is really busy tonight, so I'll make it easy and have the special one more time."

"Again, Mel? The special is all you've had since you came back to Garland Falls. How long will you stay this time?"

She shrugged. "I'm not sure. It depends on how the season goes. We've already had the first snow and not many tourists have visited. We thought the snow would help tourism pick up."

Sally sighed. "Mrs. Hall had hoped the winter carnival would bring out more people, too. If the mistletoe would arrive, I'm sure our town would get back to normal." She turned to Conner. "What would you like?"

"The special will be fine, thank you."

Conner moved his water glass to one side. "You don't live here in Garland Falls?" he said when Sally rushed off.

"Not all year round. My sister and I live in...I mean, somewhere a little north of here."

He smiled at her as he opened his straw. "I hope you'll stay at least until I finish my assessment."

"I give you my guarantee," she said. "I'll be here as long as you need my help."

He gazed at Mel until she began to fidget. "What can you tell me about the winter carnival? When does it start? How long does it last? What about it is special enough for new visitors to come to this little out of the way town?"

She breathed an inward sigh of relief when he turned to a safe topic. "The carnival starts the weekend before Christmas, which is this Sunday. It runs through January second. There are all kinds of booths with food and games. The town Christmas tree is lit on the first night of the carnival and stays on until the festivities are over. As a matter of fact, setup has already begun in the park behind the town hall."

Conner pulled out a notebook and jotted down what she told him. "Sounds like fun. What did the waitress mean about the mistletoe? Care to explain?"

Mel waited until Sally put their plates down and returned with their drinks. "The people in Garland Falls believe mistletoe possesses a special magic and it brings the town good luck. My Aunt Dee says we need its magic for the town to thrive."

"That explains the sprig she sent with her letter. I brought it back with me." He paused and looked up at her. "This town needs magic to thrive? Do you really believe mistletoe has magic?"

Mel looked at him. "I believe mistletoe is important to the town and yes, I believe in its magic. My aunt decorates the B and B with it all year round and so does everyone else in town. This is the first year we haven't been able to replace the wilted sprigs. The whole town has experienced more problems than ever. We've never not had every room booked by now, but this year, we have three families, plus my nephew."

He wrote more notes. "So, you need my agency to list Warner's B and B to attract more customers."

"You got it. If we can't get more business, my aunt and Garland Falls will suffer a lot of hardships."

They finished their dinner and stepped outside. Conner zipped up his coat and glanced up and down Main Street. "This is a nice town, but it doesn't have much to offer today's tourists," he said as he gazed in some of the shops.

"Garland Falls doesn't cater to the more expensive stores and attractions." She put her hands in her jacket pockets. "What we do have is nice and affordable for the average person."

Conner looked in the window of the small bookstore. "There's a good variety of businesses here. We might be able to build on the small, intimate shopping area for the brochure."

Mel stopped and laid her hand on his arm. "Then you think you might be able to list Warner's Bed and Breakfast and Garland Falls with your agency?"

"I'm not sure yet, but I won't make a decision until I've explored the town more."

They crossed the street in front of the town hall and walked back to his car. Mel pointed out the new leather shop, the general store, and the cookie shop. She gestured back the way they came.

"We passed Wilkerson's Garage. They're the best mechanics around. Pops is the owner and the guy who works for him got married not too long ago. We get a few new people who end up moving here, but we need more exposure. I'm sure you'll be able to help. When the mistletoe arrives, you'll see a huge turn around in the town and the B and B."

He held open the car door for her and walked around to the driver's side. "Maybe Garland Falls and Warner's would be better off to work harder to gain attention. You need a better plan than to wait for a parasitic plant which may never arrive."

Mel stared at him and had to force her mouth closed. "I know it's silly to someone like you, but the town needs the mistletoe. It's at the heart of all we hold dear. And don't call it a parasite plant, even though that is its classification."

"Tell me then, why it's so important."

"It's rather complicated to explain." She gazed out the window as he drove them back to the B and B. "Tomorrow, I'll take you to Callahan's Floral Emporium. Talk to Lucas. He can explain it better than I can. I have to pick up some bouquets for the rooms anyway."

"Good idea. I'd like to get a sense of the town and the people who live here." He glanced at her. "It looks like I'll start with the town flower shop. It's as good a place as any to begin."

****

Sunlight filled Mel's room, and she groaned as she draped her arm over her eyes. Darn Conner Andrews for his good looks and wonderful smile. The shock that ran through her when she grabbed his hand had resonated in her. She held that warm feeling close to her heart throughout the evening.

When she went to bed, she tossed and turned all night because he slipped into her thoughts and dreams. She got up and dragged herself into the shower. She and Aunt Dee had their first in depth talk with him soon. Time to get the fog out of her head so she could focus. As long as no other disasters had happened overnight, it'd be an easy day.

She dressed and hurried down to the dining room. She hoped there would still be some of Aunt Dee's warm cinnamon rolls left. Her steps slowed as she heard Conner's voice and her aunt's reply.

"Good morning," she said. "Aunt Dee, any rolls left?"

Dee held out a plate with two cinnamon rolls. "I had these two put aside and got them out of the oven when I heard you on the stairs."

"You're a life saver." She took a big bite and closed her eyes. "Mr. Andrews, have you tried these? People love what my aunt bakes."

"As a matter of fact, we were discussing her cooking when you came down." Conner smiled at her. "The food here is a big plus. Miss Dee has told me about some of the food she fixes. I think it would be good to mention it in the brochure."

Mel sat up straighter. "Wonderful."

He held his hand up. "We still need to go over what needs to be done to bring this place up to my company's standards. I need to make note of what repairs you've done and what still has to be handled."

"Oh, pish tosh," Dee said, as she waved her hand. "As soon as the mistletoe comes in, you'll see a huge difference in the place."

"As I told your niece last night, you need to concentrate more on your repairs, rather than a continued dependence on some superstition about a parasitic plant."

Before Dee could protest, Mel smiled. "Don't worry. I want to take him to Callahan's today. I can pick up the fresh bouquets for the rooms and find out if Lucas has heard any news about the mistletoe shipment."

"Lovely." Dee patted his hand. "Lucas will clear up all your questions, you'll see. You'll be able to understand why mistletoe is so important to Garland Falls."

"We'll see." Conner placed his napkin next to his plate and stood. "Shall we go to your office and get started?"

Mel smiled, trying to hide her nervousness. "Let's

get to it."

The three of them walked out of the dining room while Alex gathered the dirty dishes. Mel looked over her shoulder at her sister and frowned. If this first session didn't go well, this could be the last year for the B and B. So much rode on this first meeting, but no pressure. She groaned inwardly at her own bad joke.

Chapter Five

Mel glanced at her aunt while Conner studied the long repair list. She'd made it to remind herself of what she still needed to accomplish. Her hands shook as she held them in her lap. From the look on his face, he was unimpressed with what he saw.

"If your business is down, how do you plan to pay for these repairs?" he said.

Dee handed him the ledger. "I know travel agents don't need to see an income ledger, but I want you to have a clear picture of what we're doing here and what we're up against."

"You've got a lot of good profits that come in when you're filled to capacity," he said as he studied the numbers. "But the deficits outweigh them by a good margin. The repairs needed to bring the B and B up to Andrews Travel standards are extensive. I'm not sure, as of right now, if Warner's would be good for my company to list. You don't have enough in your account to pay for the entire list of repairs."

"I see," Mel mumbled. "I guess you can't help us, then."

He faced her and smiled. "I said 'as of right now' it's not up to our standards. I plan to be here for at least a week. I'll take some notes, make some suggestions, and let's see if I can help you out a little." He handed the ledger back to Dee. "If we do decide to add you to our listings, recommendations from my agency will boost your bottom line. You'd then have enough to accomplish every repair on your list."

She sat up straighter. "You know, at first, I didn't think Aunt Dee should've contacted you. Looks like it turned out to be a great idea after all."

He tucked his notebook into his briefcase and stood. "The town is picture perfect with the snow on the buildings and the ground. People here are friendly, and the food is good. These are all bonuses which will benefit you in the long run. I'd like to check out the winter carnival when it opens. It will a great selling point to bring the tourists to northern Minnesota."

"This afternoon, we'll go to Callahan's," she said. "You can meet Lucas and, if you're lucky, Mrs. Hall will be there. She's in charge of all the events and festivals. She can give you the rundown of all the town has to offer."

He smiled at her. "And if she's not there?"

"Then we'll go to her office, but she's always in town before the carnival. She wants to make sure the event will be perfect." Mel stood and shook his hand, once again, loving the way his large hand warmed her smaller one. "We'll head out after lunch if you like."

"Perfect."

Dee walked him to the lobby. "I'll have lunch ready for you two around one."

Mel and her aunt watched Conner walk up the stairs. "What do you think, Aunt Dee?"

"I think things have started to progress very well." She winked. "Yes. Very well indeed."

****

Conner stared out the window in his room as he

twirled the wilted sprig of mistletoe between his fingers. He'd felt different ever since he opened Dee Warner's letter and it fell into his lap. He'd wanted to throw it out but couldn't do it. How could this tiny plant affect him in such a strange way?

"Mistletoe, it would help if you could tell me why you're so special to this town," he murmured.

The thin branch shuddered for a moment, then became still again. He stared at it, not sure what happened. Did it respond to his voice, or did his hand shake and his imagination took over? As soon as the little plant responded, the itch in his brain lessened. This trip had taken a bizarre and unexpected turn. Still, he refused to give into the notion of magic.

He shook his head. The atmosphere in this little town and the B and B had started to get to him. He'd been in town once, and he already liked it more than Coco Beach. Of course, it could be the lovely Mel making him want to list the B and B. Maybe he should think about what magic she used on him to keep invading his mind. Wouldn't his mother love to hear those thoughts?

His phone rang. He rolled his eyes. Speak of the impeccably dressed and manicured devil. "Hey, Mom."

"Conner, have you made a determination about this out of the way bed and breakfast? I still don't think it will be a good fit for Andrews Travel. Why don't you forget it and come home?"

"I think it will be beneficial for us to have it in our brochures," he said as he ignored her statement. "It's a nice place, with an old world feel. It looks like what people want these days. There are several small issues to address, and I want to check out the rest of the town, but yes. I think our clients would like it here."

"Are you serious?" Her voice rose in pitch and volume. "When you got the letter, you didn't think it would be worth the trip."

Conner sighed. "No, Mom. You thought it wouldn't be worth it. New destinations are always worth any trip. You know Dad's philosophy about visits to new places. Snow has fallen here and it makes the whole town scenic, like a Christmas card. I've been into Garland Falls once, but all the stores are decorated. It all looks great, like a small town out of the 1950's."

"And what about Felicia? She'd never want to leave Coco Beach to vacation in some horrid little town," his mother snapped. "When will you come back to marry her?"

"They have a winter carnival here," he said, sidestepping the question. "I want to stay and check it out. It could be another point in the town's favor. I'll be home as soon as I can. This trip is important to me right now. It gives us a variety on our website we haven't had before."

He flinched when she hung up. As soon as she did, his phone rang again. This time, the caller ID showed his brother's name. "Hi, Michael. I guess you heard Mom as she read me the riot act?"

"I think half of Florida heard her. Tell me the truth. How is the B and B and the town so far?"

Conner wandered back over to the window. "They could be better. The B and B needs some work, but it's nice, comfortable. The town is small, but with plenty of variety in the businesses. From what I've eaten so far, the food is great. There's a lot of good points, but also some which aren't so good."

"What's not good?"

"The people here have this weird obsession with mistletoe. They think it has magic and will fix all their problems."

Michael laughed. "Magic is your big problem with Garland Falls? I think we can live with some quirkiness. Our clients would love it." He paused. "Do you still have the one Mrs. Warner sent to you?"

Conner looked at the small plant he still held. "Yeah. I can't make myself throw it away. Every time I try, it stops me."

"Maybe there's more to their obsession after all. Their superstition could have an effect on you. You never know, they might try to make you believe in its magic."

"Okay, this conversation is done. Remember, Michael. There's no such thing as magic."

"Killjoy."

After they hung up, Conner studied the mistletoe he still held. His father believed in magic, and his mother didn't. His brother believed, and he didn't. Mel believed, so did her aunt and the waitress at the diner. Who was right? Him or the people in this town? Could he be in the wrong? He scratched the back of his neck again, trying to relieve the sensation inside his head.

"Dad, you called Garland Falls quirky, but you neglected to mention their fanciful beliefs in magic."

****

As soon as they finished lunch, Mel and Conner got in her aunt's small pickup truck. "Lucas' business is about two miles outside of town," she said. "He has huge fields and a greenhouse behind his shop where he grows all the flowers he sells."

She drove them out to Lucas' store. She waited for a few minutes until a parking space opened up. She pulled in and waved to some of the folks she knew. People hurried in and out of the shop, a large variety of plants and flowers in their arms or in bags. Everyone had a smile on their face and stopped to greet or chat with others.

When they got out, Conner stared at the sign. "Callahan's Floral Emporium? Kind of a pretentious name, isn't it?"

Mel laughed and got out of the car. "Lucas likes it. He says all the cutesy flower shop names were already taken and he wanted to stand out. Come on. There's Mrs. Hall's car. I don't see any flowers in the backseat, so she should still be inside. You can meet her and make a time to go see her. She can give you a detailed rundown of the events in Garland Falls."

She opened the door and could sense him right behind her. If she were blindfolded, she'd know he was there. Even though he had scoffed at the idea of magic, she'd gotten used to having him with her. Every time he smiled at her, her insides did funny flips and twists. She'd never had such a strong reaction to any man before, not in the winter kingdom and never in Garland Falls.

Of course, they would spend a lot of time together while he stayed at the B and B. She felt positive Aunt Dee had a hand in this somewhere. Her aunt had her own kind of magic to weave, and Mel called it matchmaking. They edged their way to the counter, and she waved to the dark-haired man behind the counter as he rang up customers.

"Hi, Ray," she said. "Is Lucas around? This is

Conner Andrews. He'd like to talk to Lucas, and I need to pick up the bouquets for the B and B."

"He's in his office. We got hit with an overload of orders today." He pointed to the back. "We got the B and B's order ready as soon as we opened. Go on, Mel. He should be able to give you a few minutes of his time. This year, we're busier than ever."

"Thanks, and it's nice to see someone doing well."

She squeezed her way through the crush of people, while she dragged Conner behind her. She knocked on the office door, then pushed it open. Lucas held the phone on his shoulder while he flipped through a pile of papers on his desk. He looked up and grinned while he waved her in. She and Conner sat and waited for him to finish his call.

He threw his cell phone on the desk and leaned back in his chair. "I knew you'd be around today, Mel. What can I help you with?"

"I'm here to pick up Aunt Dee's order, and she wanted me to ask you about the mistletoe. I also wanted you to meet Conner Andrews. He's the representative from Andrews Travel we told you about last week."

Luca shook Conner's hand. "Ah, the mystery man you were at dinner with last night. Nice to meet you, Mr. Andrews."

"He's not a mystery man," Mel said, as her cheeks warmed. "He's here to see if his company should list Garland Falls and Warner's B and B. Aunt Dee hopes it will bring in more tourists and money to the town."

Lucas glanced at Conner before he turned back to Mel. "What about the one small idiosyncrasy this town requires to get here?"

"The town must have wanted him to come, or he

wouldn't have found it." Mel glanced at Conner when he frowned. "Aunt Dee thinks the new mistletoe will help with this particular quirk. So far, the town likes him, and I think it will approve of any idea he has to help. Any word yet on when the mistletoe will arrive? We've never had the winter carnival without it and attendance is down a lot from last year. The B and B isn't even close to sold out."

"I've spoken with the…" he paused, never taking his gaze from Conner. "My contacts. The harvest has been very light this year. It's strange. I'm told it's like all the mistletoe vanished overnight. They're trying to gather more from nearby king…I mean, states, but they haven't had too much luck. I hope to have a delivery by the end of the week."

"Awesome, Lucas. Aunt Dee will be happy to hear any kind of good news."

"Excuse me, Mr. Callahan," Conner said. "But I noticed you hesitated when you mentioned your distributer for the mistletoe."

"I get it from a private family farm." Lucas glanced at Mel. "They like to remain anonymous."

"I see. Can't you call another farm to get it if it's so important to the town? And it sounded like you had a different word in mind other than states. Where did you mean?"

"Nothing. A slip of the tongue, nothing more." Lucas laughed. "And I can't take a chance that I'd upset the one family I trust. No, thanks. I'll wait."

Conner made a few more notes. "I guess I can understand what you mean. Can you tell me why this particular plant is so important to this town?"

Lucas looked at Mel, who shrugged. She didn't

know how to explain it to Conner, and she kind of felt bad she had dumped this on Lucas. Still, who better to talk about plants than the guy who worked with them his whole life. Her cellphone vibrated in her pocket.

"Excuse me," she said and hurried out to the shop. "Hey, Alex, what's wrong?"

"The heat's out," Alex said. Mel could hear the tears in her voice. "I think our furnace has given up. Our few guests have said if we don't get it fixed, they'll check out early."

"Great," she sighed. "Don't panic and try to keep everyone calm. I'll be home in a few minutes to take a look at it. We may have to break down and spend some of the savings to get a new one. I'll have to cancel the order here at Callahan's. Until this happened, the flowers weren't a frivolity. Now though, I can't justify the expense."

She hung up and went back into the office. "I'm sorry, but I have to leave for a bit. There's an emergency at the B and B. Lucas, I hate to say this, but I have to cancel the bouquet order. There's a chance I have to replace the furnace."

Lucas leaned back and grinned. "Take the bouquets. Pay me whenever you can."

Conner stared at him. "You aren't worried about payment?"

"You don't get it do you, Mr. Andrews?" he said. "Garland Falls is a place where we take care of each other. If you don't learn this lesson quick, we may not be the right place for you or your company after all."

"Conner, if you'd like to stay and talk with Lucas for a bit, I shouldn't be more than an hour or so. He can give you more insight, and I can have Mrs. Hall come in and talk to you also."

"Good idea." He reached in his pocket and took out his notebook. "It will give me a better sense of what's so special about this town."

Mel hurried out and caught Mrs. Hall as she headed for the door. "Can you go to Lucas' office? There's a gentleman here who'd like some information about our town's events." She gave the older woman a sly wink. "And everyone knows, you *are* the lady to see."

"Of course, dear," she said as she patted Mel's hand. "You don't need to butter me up. I'm always happy to talk about our town's festivals." The stout, short lady hurried back into the store and headed straight for Lucas' office.

Mel loaded the bouquets in the back of the truck and hurried back to the B and B. "Please don't let this be a bigger disaster than what I know it will be," she mumbled.

Chapter Six

Mel whacked the furnace with her wrench, the metallic echo reverberating through the cellar. She leaned her head against it before she turned to her sister. "You were right, Alex. This old monstrosity is shot. I'll go see Lou about how much a new one will cost."

"We're lucky you kept it running as long as you did. You've developed a real talent for repairs."

"I picked up this particular talent out of necessity." Mel threw her tools in the toolbox and kicked the lid over. "I didn't think this old boy would make it through to the end of winter. What does Aunt Dee say?"

"What she always says. Do what you have to, and all situations will work out for the best. She went to see Mrs. C and got some complimentary quilts for the guests. She handed them out for everyone to keep, for what she calls, 'a tiny inconvenience.' I'm glad Mrs. C always has the crafters make more during the year in case of emergencies."

"This is not a tiny inconvenience," Mel said as she kicked the furnace. "If this keeps up, I may have to apprentice in the tinker realm to improve my skills. Let me get to Lou's. Maybe he knows an installer who won't charge us an arm and a leg."

Alex held up her hands. "Got my fingers crossed."

Mel got back in her aunt's truck and tried hard not

to cry. They'd had so much bad luck this year. If the mistletoe would arrive, she knew all the problems would work themselves out. She drove back to town and parked at the hardware store. Between the attack on the Hope Rose in the spring, the supernatural attack at Halloween, and now the delay with the mistletoe shipment, she felt Garland Falls' luck would run out soon. How much longer could the little town survive this kind of downturn?

****

Conner looked around the office and couldn't pin down the exact dimensions. It appeared to shrink and expand with the light. Floor to ceiling windows let daylight in behind Lucas. His desk had been positioned close to the windows and plants sat on shelves to the left and right. The empty wall to his left puzzled him. He thought there would have been pictures or maybe a bookcase there. On top of Lucas' desk were piles of papers, but he couldn't see a computer.

As the sunlight shone into the room, out of the corner of his eye, Conner could swear he saw a yellow door fade in and out on the empty wall. The vision depended on how the light angled. He turned his head and stared at the open space. He could almost see the outline of a doorway before the light shifted and the wall turned plain once more.

He cleared his throat and tapped his small notebook. "I'd like you to tell me why mistletoe is so important to Garland Falls. Mel said you could explain better than she could."

Lucas threw his black cowboy hat on his desk and knocked over a pile of invoices. "It's difficult to pin down why it's so important, but I'll do my best.

Garland Falls always has mistletoe throughout the year. The first place my brother hangs it is at the B and B, since he works there. From the top of the hill, it's like magic flows down to the town. Of course, all the shops have at least one sprig in there somewhere. However, the bigger the store, the more sprigs the store will need. The town elders believe the mistletoe's magic gives the town good luck and protects it from outside forces."

Conner bit his lip, to stop himself from making a negative comment. But really, magic again? Isn't there any place he could go to get away from all this nonsense? "So, everyone in Garland Falls believes in magic and thinks this parasitic plant can protect them? And what outside forces do you mean? Are there gangs or criminals nearby?"

"Nothing so pedestrian as regular bad guys." Lucas chuckled. "I'm sure you'll hear stranger stories about the town while you're here. I can't deny that when we don't get the mistletoe shipment on time, the town has a run of bad luck." He turned to Mrs. Hall. "You've been very quiet, ma'am. Did you want to add to this conversation?" He grinned. "You know you love to have a say in important topics."

"I've heard quite enough out of you, Mr. Lucas Callahan. I don't need your sass this afternoon. I have enough on my plate as it is." She laid her hand on Conner's arm. "Melissa said you wanted to know about our events. Let's go back to my office and I'll see if I can tell you what you want to know." She glared at Lucas, but smiled, too. "We could use a little peace and quiet."

"Are you sure you have time right now?" Conner said. "Mel made it clear you're very busy with the carnival. I wouldn't want to keep you from your work."

"It's not work if you enjoy what you do," she said as she stood. "It won't take any time at all to show you what we have planned. Let's go to my office."

Lucas stood when they did. He shook Conner's hand again. "Come back any time you have questions. I'll help you out as much as I can."

Conner followed Mrs. Hall out to her small sedan and climbed in the passenger seat. Lucas ended his questions when he turned the discussion over to the stout, smiling lady next to him. He settled back for the ride to her office. There would be time enough to get the answers he needed from the residents of this town.

After all, he couldn't help them if he didn't have all the information. He stared out the window. This town had secrets, but were they good secrets or bad ones? On the surface, Garland Falls seemed too good to be true. But what lurked beneath the pleasant facade? He'd learned a long time ago, if it sounded too good to be true, don't trust it.

****

"Lou," Mel called out as she entered the hardware store. "I'm in desperate need of serious help."

Lou came out of the back room and walked behind the counter. "I guess this isn't the social visit we talked about when you were here last. Tell me what's happened this time."

"The furnace is completely shot," she said. She tried hard to keep the tremors out of her voice. "We have guests who will leave if we don't get it repaired pronto. Please tell me you can help."

"Does it need to be fixed or replaced like I told you the last time you came here about it?"

She sighed. "We need a replacement. The one we have lasted on a wing and a prayer and that was about it. Do you have one and can you recommend a cheap installer? Money's gotten tight and this will set us back even farther."

"I did warn you when you came here about a repair the last time it wouldn't last." Lou handed her a piece of candy. "You aren't a miracle worker, even if you do have a talent for complicated repairs."

"Don't rub it in. I'm at my wit's end." She ate the candy and swallowed hard. "Aunt Dee's B and B has had more and more problems crop up the longer it takes to get the new mistletoe."

He patted her hand. "Now, don't you worry, Mel. I already ordered one because I knew you'd need it sooner rather than later. I know a guy who can help you out. He's from the tinker realm."

"Oh, no. Not the tinker realm." She narrowed her eyes. "I'll tell you right now, I refuse to owe him a favor. They're notorious for their unreasonable demands."

"No, no, no. The person I have in mind wouldn't place an unreasonable demand on you. You know Isaac down at the garage?" He smiled when she nodded. "It's his brother, Tristan. Trust me. Isaac and Pops won't let him bully you and don't you worry about the cost."

Mel wiped her eyes. "Everyone has been so generous to us."

"Christmas always brings out the best in people. Consider all this as a present for Dee." He walked around the counter and hugged her. "This town owes Miss Dee and the B and B a lot. She's always been there for everyone in town. The people here wouldn't know what to do without her. We're happy to be of help. I'll deliver the new furnace this afternoon and Tristan will be there in the morning."

"Awesome. Thanks, Lou. I'll let Aunt Dee know. She'll be happy to hear some good news for a change."

Mel headed to the grocery store. May as well pick up some items so she wouldn't have to make another trip later. She could wrap up a few errands while she waited for Conner to finish up with Lucas and Mrs. Hall. She could walk around town until he was done, and looked forward to sitting in the car with him on the ride back to the B and B.

****

Mrs. Hall sat behind her desk and folded her hands on top of a pile of paper. "Now, Mr. Andrews, how can I help you? You indicated an interest in our town's festivals."

Conner adjusted himself on the chair in front of her desk. Why did everyone he met have huge piles of paper on their desks? "I'd like to know about the events you have here. What about them is special enough to draw tourists? In other words, why should my company add Garland Falls to our travel listings?"

"Very good questions, sir." Mrs. Hall mumbled to herself as looked through the stack on her desk. "Ah ha," she cried as she pulled out one sheet from the tallest stack. "This is the list of planned events for next year. Each festival is unique to its own particular season. We have food and games, special to each holiday."

He took out his notebook and clicked his pen. "Can you give me some examples?"

She tapped her chin. "Well, the winter carnival has

started its set up right now. It will open on Sunday. It runs from the week before Christmas until January 2. Once the town tree is lit, it's never turned off until the carnival is over." She winked at him. "Valentine's Day has its own special party, and we celebrate the vernal equinox when a special rose blooms. I could go on and on about what we have planned, but you have all the information there."

Conner made notes and frowned. "How can a town this small afford to put on all these festivals? This sounds expensive to hold all year long." He wondered again at what secrets the town hid. If he asked Mrs. Hall, what would she say?

"They are a bit expensive, but we have a lot of volunteers, and the townspeople donate a lot of items." She gave him a warm smile, as her eyes twinkled with delight. "We haven't missed a celebration ever." She leaned forward. "We believe these events bring people closer together. They foster community, you see, and help those who need it most. It's why they're so important. After all, isn't that why we're here? To celebrate and help those who could use help and maybe some goodwill? They should know they aren't forgotten souls."

"Yes, ma'am, I suppose so. I've never met such a close-knit community before. I think my clients would like to spend some time here. Maybe Garland Falls will remind them of what's important. Can I hold onto this list?" When she agreed, he stood and tucked the list into his notebook. "If you don't mind, I'd like to walk around the town and get a feel for it. I need to see what else is special enough to draw our clientele here."

She stood and walked around her desk. "I'll be

happy to drop you off. I need to go to Heavenly Bites and make sure my cookie order will be delivered on time." She smiled and took his arm. "My event committee gets cranky if we don't have our cookies and Heavenly Bites has the most delectable cookies around."

He held the door open and followed her out. She chattered on the whole short drive to the small cookie shop on Main Street. Conner unhooked his seatbelt and started to get out when Mrs. Hall laid her hand on his arm. "Mr. Andrews, I detect a strong disbelief in magic in you."

"You're right. My father believed and my brother does, but I'm afraid it would take a lot to convince me magic is real."

She patted his arm. "By the time you leave Garland Falls, I think you'll believe in all kinds of magic. Who knows? You may even discover some magic inside yourself. Enjoy your explorations."

Conner stood on the sidewalk and watched her enter Heavenly Bites. What did she mean? He'd never believed and never would. What did she mean about magic inside him? He knew it couldn't be true. He walked down the street and tried to banish her words from his mind. As he did, he felt movement in his pocket and the itchy sensation in his mind once again.

Chapter Seven

"Conner."

He looked up and saw Mel wave. He waited while she hurried to him. "Hello, Mel. I thought you headed back to the B and B."

She huffed out a sigh. "I did, but I had to come see about a new furnace. Ours is shot."

He took out his notebook and wrote in it. He tucked it back in his pocket and looked around. "I'm sorry. Will it be fixed in time for your winter carnival?"

"It should be functional by tomorrow." She sighed. "There's a guy from…a repair company who can help me. He can work magic with repairs."

He gazed at the stores and noticed the wilted sprigs of mistletoe. "Does this whole town believe in magic?"

She started at his question, as she realized what she'd said. "Yes. It's part of our charm."

"Even you?" He shook his head as he started to walk away. "Magic isn't real, you know."

"It could be." She took small, quick steps to keep pace with his longer stride. "You have a pretty narrow-minded view of the world. Why don't you believe magic could exist? Didn't you ever read fairy tales?"

Why didn't he? His father had a strong belief in magic and his brother did as well. So why did he take after his mother's view when he'd spent most of his time with his dad? Why didn't his father's faith in magic carry over to him, like it did with his brother?

"Because I run a multi-million-dollar business, which pushed any fanciful notions out of me," he said. "I need to be practical about what I do, day in and day out. I don't have time for fairy tales, monsters, or magic. Look at you. You believe in magic and yet your aunt's B and B is in serious need of help."

"True, but fairy tales are more real than you think, and some monsters are pretty nice once you get to know them." She grinned. "You have a pretty judgmental attitude, Mr. Andrews."

He couldn't help but smile back. "Maybe I do. Do you think you can change my mind?" He pulled her arm through his as they walked down the street. "I'll listen to any sensible argument you might have. Like how you know monsters are nice."

"I'm afraid I'll have to tell you the monster story another day. I do like a good argument on occasion. Be prepared, though." She squeezed his arm. "I might be able to persuade you to our way of thinking, even though it might not be as sensible as you'd like it to be, Mr. Andrews."

"I'll take my chances, Miss Owens." He smoothed back a stray strand of her hair when she looked up at him. "You should also be prepared. You might come around to my way of thinking instead."

"Maybe. Maybe not," she said, then cleared her throat. "Let's see how far the carnival setup has progressed. Most of the booths should be almost done by now. You can get a sense of what the finished project will look like."

"Sounds good. Let's go."

He had to admit to himself, Garland Falls did have

a certain charm, and so did the woman who walked next to him. She led him back down to the town hall and took him on the narrow sidewalk around to the park behind it. Some booths were half finished, some were completely finished, and some were in the early stages.

"How long does the carnival set up take?" he said.

Mel waved to a few people. "Not long. Since the booths are run by the shop keepers, most of the work is done at night when the stores close." She pointed to a booth in the middle of the row. "The booth over there is for the Heavenly Bites shop. Davin and Joanna will be back here around six to finish it. The one over there is for the new leather store which opened at the start of November."

"They work out here at night in the cold?"

She laughed. "Yep, even when it snows. Sometimes, we even have a good snowball fight, to lighten the mood. People wouldn't stop for mere cold to make sure the carnival is a success."

"They sure are dedicated." Conner looked around at the few people who worked on their booths. Most laughed with others, and he felt they didn't consider this work at all. "Does your aunt have a booth here?"

Mel shook her head. "No. She's too busy at the B and B to have a booth. My sister, Alex, wants to set one up this year if they have space. I believe she's already spoken to Mrs. Hall about it."

"Good idea. She could sell some of your aunt's food. Her cinnamon rolls would help bring in more revenue for you." He stopped and turned her to him. "How far north of Garland Falls do you live?"

"It's hard to explain. Like Garland Falls, where I'm from is a small town, more of a village. Alex and I come here for the occasional visit."

He folded his arms as he stared at her. "Would you like to tell me where?"

"I don't think so."

"Why not?"

She shrugged. "You wouldn't believe me. You might even consider me crazy. I don't want to prejudice you against Aunt Dee or Garland Falls because of what I might say or do."

He smiled. "Try me. I promise I'll keep an open mind."

"Okay." She took a deep breath. "Once upon a time, two princesses from the winter kingdom came to a small town in Minnesota to help out their aunt with her B and B. The sisters have to go back after Christmas to choose their consorts. After they find their perfect match, they'll be married. The end."

He stood in shocked silence and the minutes stretched out. "You're kidding."

"Maybe yes, maybe no." She walked toward the end of the row where some of the other food booths were set up. "Okay, yes, you got me. It's a silly story I made up. My sister and I live with our parents in a small town a little farther north. It's over the Canadian border."

"Uh, huh." He walked next to her and put his arm around her shoulders. "Next you'll tell me Santa Claus is real."

She smiled as she gazed at him. "You know the song, right? You'd better not shout and you'd better not cry." Then she laughed. "Wouldn't it be nice if Santa were real? Think of all the good which could happen when you believe. So, yes. I believe with all my heart

Santa Claus is real."

"I see."

"I knew you'd call me crazy." She ducked out from underneath his arm and turned to head back to her car. She sensed Conner right behind her as he hurried to catch up. "It doesn't matter if you believe me or not. There is magic in Garland Falls. Because we haven't gotten the mistletoe, a lot of people and businesses have had a lot of problems. Its magic is needed here. When it comes, you'll be surprised at how much brighter the town will be. We may even get the huge influx of tourists we usually have."

"Mel, I didn't call you crazy. Please listen to me for a minute," he said as he turned her to face him. "I knew this town had secrets, but I didn't expect them to be this outlandish."

"I suppose we are different than what you expected. We keep secrets until we know a person can be trusted. The town has decided to wait to see if you deserve our trust." She glanced down, then back up at him. "Does this change your opinion about listing us with your agency?"

He leaned closer to her and tilted her head back. "Not in the least. People like eccentric small-town folks."

"I see," she said. Her breath caught in her throat as her body trembled. Was it possible he would kiss her right now, right here? "I suppose eccentric could be good in this case."

He lowered his head another inch as her eyes drifted closed. He stopped and stepped back as he scratched at the back of his neck. "We'd better go to the B and B. We don't want to worry Miss Dee."

"Right."

They got in her car, and she blasted the heat. The bright blue sky didn't have a cloud in sight, and the sun shone on the snow and made it sparkle like gems in the bright light. When they arrived at the B and B, he got out and stared at the Victorian house before he turned back to look at the town.

"Don't stay out here too long," Mel said. "Snow should arrive in the next hour or so."

"But it's clear," he said, as he gazed upward at the cerulean sky. "How do you know it will snow?"

"Call it winter pixie intuition." She grinned and wiggled her fingers at him. "Or maybe I can summon storms with the magic power I carry inside me."

He didn't know whether to laugh at her or take her seriously. When she told him the story about the two sisters who were winter pixies, she appeared to be completely honest. Could she and her sister be real pixies from another kingdom? His stomach soured at the thought of her choosing someone else and not him to be her consort. He watched her go inside and shivered when a cold wind sprung up out of nowhere. He looked up at the sky and noticed clouds had started to gather.

The gray clouds framed the three-story Victorian bed and breakfast. It almost looked like it belonged in some spooky movie. The white paint with green trim and green shutters had the look of a fairy tale home. The gray, wrap-around porch with its rockers on each side of the front door appeared to be the epitome of coziness.

The groundskeeper, Parker, he remembered, did a wonderful job with the decorations. A huge wreath hung on the front door, and smaller ones adorned the windows. Garland draped from the railing, and bunches of red winterberries made a nice contrast against the dark green and the snow.

Medium planters lined the steps to the porch and contained small, white flowers which almost looked like roses. The Christmas tree in the drawing room shone bright in the window. Why should it be so hard for him to give in to the belief in magic? This whole town almost reeked of magic.

He thought about Mel and all she'd told him. Of course, with her trim figure and crystal-clear blue eyes, she resembled a pixie in more ways than one. His father had told him stories of winter pixies and their ability to predict when snow would come. He didn't believe those stories when he'd heard them as a boy, and even less when he became an adult.

Of course, he'd heard them long before he'd met Delia Warner and a certain Miss Melissa Owens.

Chapter Eight

"This whole town is nuts," Conner said when he called his brother. "Maybe you should've been the one who came up here instead of me."

Michael laughed. "You know I can't be objective where magic is concerned. I have Dad's faith in magic and maybe some faith of my own. You also don't sound as sure as you did before."

"Don't start with me, Michael. I wish I did have some of yours and Dad's faith. It would make it easier to get along with the people here." Conner pushed the curtain aside and stared at the falling snow. "I didn't think she'd be right, but she is. It's started to snow."

"Who was right?"

He dropped the curtain and walked over to the bed and sat. "Melissa Owens. About ninety minutes ago, she told me it would snow, and now it is."

"She must have heard the weather report."

"She couldn't have," Conner said. "We were together for most of the afternoon. She looked at a clear sky and said it would snow."

"Okay, how did she know?"

He ran a hand through his hair. "I have no idea. She also told me some strange fairy tale, about being a winter pixie. She implied she's also a princess. How am I supposed to react to this? She's as human as you and I." He huffed out a sigh. "And princesses, from what I understand, don't go around fixing appliances and holding tarantulas."

"You never know. She might be." Michael laughed again. "You are so uptight. Just roll with it. It shouldn't matter if she says she's some kind of supernatural creature. If you like her, does it matter what she says or believes?"

"Yes, it matters," he almost shouted. "If the one person I considered normal says she's some kind of fairy, can the rest of this town be any different? We can't recommend our clients to come to a town full of strange people." He got up to pace around the room. "Maybe I should say this won't work for us and come home."

"Conner, don't you dare give up. First of all, Mom will lord it over you for the rest of your life. You know how she feels about your trip up there. Dig a little deeper. Talk to more people."

His brother had a point, but he had to add on, "She also acts like Santa Claus is real. You don't think she's crazy?"

Michael fell silent for a moment. "Oh, come on, Conner. Lots of people, and I mean lots of adults, still believe Santa is real. You sure she didn't mean some guy dressed up as Santa at a shopping center or mall?"

"She didn't talk about any mall Santa," Conner said. "There's no mall nearby. No national chain stores, no chain restaurants. Heck, I haven't even seen one computer. At least they have cell phones. Every business here in this town is family owned and incredibly retro."

"And they all believe in magic."

"Right." Conner frowned when his brother laughed

again. "I don't know why I called you. You've been absolutely no help."

He hung up and lay back on the bed. A bouquet of fresh flowers adorned the dresser, their fragrance filling the air. He breathed deep, and let the scent calm him. Why did her revelations upset him so much? He thought about it for a long time. Maybe because deep down inside, he wanted to believe what she told him as absolute truth.

He thought about what his brother said. What did it matter what she and the rest of the residents of Garland Falls believed? He liked Melissa Owens and had almost let himself kiss her. He also had started to like this small town in the middle of nowhere Minnesota. He admitted to himself he wanted to list Garland Falls. He wanted his clients to get to know this tiny town. He liked being here, and his new fondness included the residents. He liked Mel more than he believed possible and his like for her grew deeper every day.

He remembered one of their earlier conversations and smiled to himself. She sure had him pegged as narrow-minded. Could it be possible his mother had influenced him more than he thought? He thought about how his father looked at his mother, like she was the one woman in the world for him. If he did believe in magic, it had been in their marriage. Maybe one day he'd have a special kind of magic like that for himself.

****

"You told him what we are?" Alex said. Shock and disbelief colored her words. "How could you tell him the truth? More important, what did he say?"

"I made it sound like a child's story. Right now, I'm sure he thinks I'm some kind lunatic." Mel folded her arms on the dining room table and laid her head on them. "How could I be so stupid? I even implied I believed in Santa, and we both know he and Mrs. C are real. What if he decides not to list the B and B? How could I tell Aunt Dee it would be all my fault?"

"You know what Mom and Aunt Dee always say. Don't borrow trouble." Alex stroked her sister's hair. "Trust he won't make any rash decisions because you spilled the beans about our pixie heritage."

Mel raised her head. "Alex, I can fix plumbing, broken stairs, and find a lost tarantula. So, tell me. How can I fix this?"

"I don't think you can." They both stared at the ceiling when they heard a bang. "But whatever happened, I think your repair talents are needed once more."

Mel pushed to her feet. "Of course. I swear you'd think I came from the tinker realm and couldn't be a princess of the winter court."

Alex covered her mouth and opened her eyes wide. "You didn't tell him we were royalty, too, did you?"

"I implied it in the story I sort of made up. I didn't blurt it right out." She frowned as she left the dining room. "If I dropped such a huge bombshell on him, he would have left Garland Falls and never returned."

Mel hurried to the stairs and rushed to the second floor. The few guests they had were in the hallway as they looked up and down. "Does anyone know where the bang came from?" she asked.

"We heard it in the room at the end of the hall," one guest said.

She sighed and headed down the hall. "It's okay, everyone. I know the room and there isn't any problem.

I'll take care of what happened."

She opened the door and closed it behind her. Bobby stood in the middle of the room, hands on his hips, and a frown on his face. "Fred, you come out right now," he said, as he stamped his foot.

The huge book Alex had put on top of the terrarium lay on the floor. The tarantula shouldn't have been able to knock it off. What had gotten into the spider? If no new mistletoe had made pets act up, she would throw in the towel right now.

"I guess Fred decided to escape again?" she said.

"What am I going to do, Mel?" Bobby stared at her while his bottom lip trembled. "He's never been this strong before."

"I guess he's gotten into some kind of super spider food." She looked around the room. "He didn't get out of here, did he?" The boy shook his head. "Let's go find him. Maybe if we talk to him, he'll stop all these escape attempts."

Mel found the tarantula under the bed. She coaxed him to her hand and sat on the floor and gestured for Bobby to do the same. "Now listen, Fred. You have to stop climbing out of your home. We keep you in there to make sure you're safe. How would Bobby feel if he lost you for good? You know he'd miss you. And it's cold outside. You'd never be able to live out there."

"Please listen to her, Fred," Bobby said while he stroked the tarantula. "I don't want to lose you."

"She's right, Fred," Conner said from the doorway. He came over and sat on the floor next to Mel. "I know you get out because you can, but it doesn't mean you should. Now be a good tarantula and stay in your terrarium."

The spider turned to Conner and appeared to cock his head. He gave the impression of a shrug and walked back to the dresser, climbed up the side and back into his terrarium. The three of them got off the floor and the boy threw his arms around Conner's legs.

"Thank you. I knew he needed an adult to tell him to be good."

Mel and Conner left the room and shut the door behind them. Mel walked down the stairs in front of him. She went into the drawing room and sat in one of the wingback chairs. Conner sat across from her, and they stared at each other.

"How can you talk to spiders?" she said.

"I followed your lead." He leaned forward. "Are you going to spout more magic mumbo jumbo at me?"

"Of course not. You've made your opinion quite clear." She stared at the fire. "I shouldn't have told you what I did. Don't let my lame story color your opinion of the B and B and Garland Falls. I know we look and act a bit odd, but we're a regular town."

"A regular town," he repeated. "A town which has to like a person to allow them to be here."

"People do say you have to have magic in you to even find the town."

He laughed at her statement. "Are you serious? I found it on my GPS. It's a little out of the way, but it popped right up when I put in the address for the B and B."

She shrugged. "Garland Falls must have a reason for wanting you here."

"Maybe it does. Maybe it wants some good old-fashioned reality."

Now she took her turn to laugh. "Reality is

overrated. Don't you even want to try to believe in magic?"

"I guess I'm too practical for magic."

Dee walked in with a tea tray. "I thought you two might like a light snack. Alex made some fresh sourdough bread, and I brought some of my homemade raspberry jam."

"Thanks, Aunt Dee. Fred got out again. I swear Bobby's tarantula is stronger than he used to be. I may have to make a terrarium with a locked lid."

"He won't get out again," Conner said as he spread jam on a warm slice of bread. "He told me he'll behave from now on."

Dee and Mel stared at him. "He told you?" Mel said.

Conner stopped and stared at them. "Yeah."

"He spoke to you, and you could understand him?" Dee said. "You have a wonderful, rare talent. I know a few people with those skills and let's say, they like to keep to themselves."

"I think I'll eat my bread and drink my tea." He concentrated on the slice of bread before he poured himself a cup of hot tea. "I wanted to make Bobby happy, and I guess I did."

Dee sat next to him. "Who are your parents?"

"Silas and Katherine Andrews. My father passed away about two years ago. My brother and I took over the business side of Andrews Travel while our mother handles the social engagements for our clients."

"I knew your name sounded familiar. I remember your father." Dee tapped her chin. "He lived in Garland Falls and was a very dear friend." She smiled as Conner stared at her. "You have ties here and it explains why you could find the town with ease. Now I know all will work out fine." She patted his hand and rose. "It's a real pleasure to have you here in my home."

Mel and Conner watched her leave the room, while she hummed a Christmas carol. He stared at Mel. "Do you have any idea what she meant?"

"Nope. I love my aunt, but she has a tendency to never explain herself if she doesn't want to. She also has her reasons when she keeps information to herself."

"I can't wait to find out what her reasons are for those particularly vague statements."

Chapter Nine

Mel stood in the driveway while Tristan grabbed his tools out of his truck. "Lou had the furnace delivered yesterday," she said. "I'm glad you could come install it on such short notice."

"Not a problem," he said. "I don't have a lot to do right now at home. I'm glad to help you and Miss Dee out, Mel."

They entered the basement and walked over to the far corner where the new furnace waited to be installed. Mel helped him turn off the gas and disconnect the line. Together, they moved the old furnace out and wrestled the new one into place. After all the connections had been hooked up, Mel called upstairs.

"Alex, turn on the thermostat," she shouted.

"Okay. Give me a second."

Tristan wiped the loose dirt off his hands with a towel he pulled from his back pocket. "Your sister is here?"

"Yes, she is. Do you want me to have her come down and say hi?"

Tristan put his tools away and took more care than normal to make sure they were all in the right place. "No, no. I mean, if she's not busy, I might go say hi."

Mel smiled. Tristan liked her sister. She glanced at the cellar's ceiling and then at Tristan. Aunt Dee didn't have to matchmake them. They'd done it themselves.

"Since we were told not to pay you, how about some lunch. Alex made the best sourdough bread, and we have some lunchmeat. Sound good to you?"

"It sounds great. My stomach let me know it's time for some food." He checked the new furnace one more time. "It sounds fine, so we can call it a day."

"Awesome. Let's head upstairs. I'm sure Alex and Aunt Dee have started lunch."

They walked into the kitchen, and Alex turned and dropped the butter knife she'd taken out of the drawer. Mel and Dee shared a secret smile as Tristan and Alex gazed at each other.

"I asked Tristan to stay for lunch," Mel said.

"Hi, Tristan," Alex said. "We're glad to have you join us. I'll set another place."

"If it's not too much trouble."

"Not at all." She opened the cabinet and carried another plate and silverware to the dining room. "I'll be back in a minute."

Mel hurried after her sister. "I think he likes you, and I'm pretty sure you like him as much."

"What? No, he doesn't and no, I don't. This is a polite lunch to thank him for his help."

Mel took the plate and silverware from Alex. "You can fool yourself, little sister, but not me. He likes you and you like him. Admit it."

Alex took it all back and laid it on the table. "I will, if you admit you like Conner."

"So, blackmail is the name of this game, is it?" She grinned when Alex nodded. "Okay. I like Conner. A lot." She leaned over the table and whispered to her sister, "He almost kissed me the other night."

"No way," Alex whispered back. "I'd die if Tristan

kissed me. He's so…so…"

"Exactly." They let out dreamy sighs at the same time, then giggled. "We'd better get back in the kitchen before they come looking for us," Mel said.

"Did you ask Conner to join us for lunch?" Dee asked when they walked back in.

"Not yet. Tristan and I just finished up with the new furnace," Mel said. "I'll go invite him. After all, we need to make a good impression and we can with all the great food you two make."

She hurried up the stairs, then made herself slow down when she got to his door. She took a deep breath, smoothed her hair and her clothes, then knocked. When he opened the door, her mouth went dry, and she stared at him. He'd unbuttoned his shirt, and his tousled, damp light brown hair on his head had turned a shade darker.

"Can I help you, Mel?"

She swallowed hard and forced out a smile. "We have lunch ready and wanted to know if you'd like to join us."

"Sure. Let me finish up. It won't take me long to get ready. Come on in," he said as he walked back into the bathroom. "Did you get the new furnace installed?"

Mel stepped over the threshold slowly and stood by the dresser. "Tristan and I finished up a few minutes ago and it runs like a dream. The B and B should warm up any time now."

"Great. The new quilt is nice, but there's no substitute for actual heat."

Mel looked around at his possessions in the room. He'd planned well for the cold weather, didn't like ties, and liked comfortable boots and shoes. He didn't follow fashion trends of high society; instead he went for practical. He didn't have the image of the high-end social elite he said he represented. The more she got to know him, the more down to earth he appeared to be.

She smiled as a devilish thought hit her. Maybe she'd put a small magical item in here and see if he liked it. Maybe not. She didn't want to push the little bit of luck she had left. She noticed the little sprig of mistletoe her aunt had sent to him on the nightstand. How nice he'd kept it. She looked closer at it. Did it look healthier than when Aunt Dee sent it?

He came out of the bathroom, hair brushed, shirt buttoned up (darn it), and he had grabbed a sweat-jacket. "I'm ready. Shall we go downstairs?"

She led the way back to the dining room and the others had already seated themselves. Mel noticed Tristan had taken the chair next to Alex, with Dee at the head of the table. Conner held her chair out for her and sat beside her.

"Tristan?" Conner said. When the other man nodded, he continued. "Thank you for coming out today to get the new furnace installed. I'm sure Miss Dee appreciates it as much as her guests do."

"You're welcome, and like I told Mel, my pleasure. I had no work at my shop at the moment, so I'm glad I could come help. Alex invited me to stay for lunch. I love her sourdough bread."

Conner made a sandwich. "I agree. I told Mel and Miss Dee the food here is a great way to attract more tourists. I plan to make sure the food gets its own page on our website." He turned to Mel. "If it's possible, I would like you to start a website for the B and B. The mayor should have one for the town, too."

Dee laughed. "It'll be a challenge to get that old

goat to agree to technology."

"If you want to draw in more people, you need to have an online presence these days. Most people use websites to book vacations."

"I like the sound of that," Tristan said. "I'd like to know how it works. Could you show me how to make one? I'd like to help, and I learn quickly."

"Sure. Let me know when you're available." Conner turned back to Miss Dee. "Do you know if you have WiFi here?"

"I don't think so. I'm sure you've noticed we don't have computers."

"I noticed. Computers would make a lot of your paperwork easier to handle." Conner ate his sandwich while he thought. "Garland Falls looks like it exists in a different time than the rest of the world."

"We've tried to have internet access, but we could never get the signal to come in very strong, so we gave up," Mel said.

"I'll make a note and check into how to get WiFi here." Conner pulled out his notebook and wrote in it. "A lot of our clients are business people who don't like to be out of touch with their companies for very long."

Dee winked at him. "Maybe if they were, they'd be less stressed when they got back to their lives."

"You might be right. There aren't many places for people to go to unplug from their lives. This could be another point in your favor." He paused. "How do you get cell phone signals?"

"There's a tower right down the road," Mel said. "You can see it if you go about a mile out of town to the east."

Conner grinned. "I thought for sure you would say

magic."

"Ha, ha, ha. Electronic magic is a whole different type," Mel said. "If you didn't know it before, you know it now."

"She's right," Alex said. "Tristan, do you know anyone who does electric magic?"

He shrugged. "Not off the top of my head, but I can make some calls."

Conner looked at the small group. "I don't know if you all are kidding me or not, but if it helps get WiFi here, go for it."

They finished lunch and Mel and Conner stood at the same time. "Would you like to take a walk around the grounds?" she asked. "I don't think you've seen the whole property yet."

"No, I haven't. There's a lot more snow out there than last night. I think I'd better put on my higher boots."

They got ready and Mel led him out the front door and down the steps. "In the spring, Parker, our groundskeeper, plants all kinds of different flowers around the foundation. Come out back."

She took his hand, and they walked around the house to the backyard. She pointed to a small shed in the far corner of the yard. "Parker keeps all his lawn equipment in there. See the gazebo there in the middle of the yard?" He nodded. "He built it for the guests. He married the woman who runs the leather shop in town there."

"It's a beautiful place for a wedding." He walked over to it and laid his hand on the rail and pushed. "It's a solid structure. He must be handy with tools."

"He learned from his father. He says if he didn't do

his best, his father would never let him hear the end of it." Mel stood next to him. "If you ask me, I think he likes to show off his skills."

"What about you, Mel?" he said. "What are your special skills?"

"As of right now, I can fix broken appliances, plumbing, and find lost pet tarantulas."

He leaned against the rail. "I mean, do you have a job? What do you do for a living?"

"I help out my parents and they give me money." She gave him a gentle nudge. "I get by."

"Does your aunt pay you to help out here?"

She shook her head. "Alex and I volunteered this year. We know Aunt Dee has enough to worry about. We told her not to pay us."

They continued to stroll close to the woods around the property. "Everyone I've met is too good to be true," he said.

"What do you mean?"

He shook his head. "I mean, everyone is so generous with their time and their goods."

Mel kicked at a snowdrift. "We're a community. It's what we do. Don't people care about each other in Florida?"

"Not like this." He stopped and looked around. "I'm glad I came here. I wish I didn't have to go back."

"You can stay a little longer after the winter carnival, can't you?"

He turned to face her. "I wish I could, but I have a business to run. I can't leave my brother alone too long."

She brushed his hair off his forehead. "You're a very kind person, Conner Andrews. I'm glad I've gotten to know you."

"Same here."

He leaned forward and gave her a light kiss. A quick, stiff breeze shoved Mel into his arms. She smiled and shrugged. He returned the gesture and held her close.

"This is what Christmas should feel like," she whispered.

"Yes, it is."

Chapter Ten

He'd taken the plunge and kissed Melissa Owens. Strange how he'd thought about it when the breeze came along and pushed her into his arms. He thought back to the moments before. His thoughts had turned to how pretty the trees were covered with snow and how beautiful Mel looked standing there.

Mel was the perfect complement to the scene. Sunlight shone on her honey-brown hair, and the snow glittered in the afternoon light. She fit the environment perfectly. Could she be a winter pixie? He shook his head and walked over to where the sprig of mistletoe lay.

He picked it up and stared at it as he held it in the palm of his hand. "I wish you'd talk to me like Fred did. How did I even understand it?" He began to pace. "I mean, it's not like it's the first time this has happened to me." He stopped. But this was the first time he ever admitted his hidden abilities out loud. "The urge to talk to not only people but to animals and plants, it's stronger here." He sighed as he looked again at the sprig. "And now I've decided to converse with a dying plant who understands me."

The mistletoe quivered against his palm. He brought it closer to his face. As his breath fanned over it, the leaves looked brighter, and the white berries glowed with an interior light. He blew over it again and the leaves turned a brighter green as the white berries swelled with health. He stroked the leaves until they almost burst with new growth.

"Oh, boy." He tucked the sprig in his pocket and hurried downstairs. "Mel, I have to go out for a bit. Would you like to meet me at the diner around six thirty for dinner?"

"Um, sure. I'll get there before the crowd and get us a booth." She stopped and stared at him. "Is there a problem?"

"I don't think so, but I need to have a conversation with someone."

He slipped on the fresh snow as he rushed to his car. He drove back to Callahan's Floral Emporium. Lucas knew plants and intimated he knew some about magic. Why did all this weird stuff have to happen to him, of all people, and why now? He lived in reality and had no time for dreams, fantasies, or fairy tales.

He slowed when he got to the nursery and pulled into the first space which opened up. Callahan's lot had to be the most crowded lot in the whole town. There were more cars than the last time he'd come here. He made his way in and Ray stood behind the counter, waiting on a long line of customers.

"Is Mr. Callahan here?"

"He's always here at this time of year." Ray grinned. "It doesn't hurt he lives right next door. Go on back to his office. He knew you'd stop by this afternoon."

Conner pushed his way through the throngs of people to the back of the store. He knocked on the office door and went in when Lucas hollered to do so. If possible, the mound of papers on his desk had increased to five times what it had been before. Lucas held the phone to his ear while he rummaged through the stack. He pulled out a slip, read a few numbers off, then hung up.

Lucas stood and shook Conner's hand. "Good to see you again, Mr. Andrews. I expected you about fifteen minutes ago. What can I help you with?"

Conner frowned a little. Lucas expected him earlier? Okay, he was a bit unnerved to hear he'd been expected. "You look a little busy at the moment. Is now a good time?"

"It's always like this around here. Pick any season and I'm buried under a mountain of papers. Any time is a good time."

They both sat and Conner held out the sprig of mistletoe, which had sprouted a few new leaves on the drive here. "I wondered if you could help me explain what happened to this mistletoe."

Lucas took it and stared at it. "It looks healthy. Where did it come from and what can you tell me about it?"

"Dee Warner sent this in her initial letter to me. It was almost dead, well, I mean, it was dead. The leaves were brittle, and the berries had shriveled up."

"Okay, but it looks fine now."

Conner leaned forward. "Here's where the weirdness comes in. I talked to it, then I breathed on it, and now it's healthy. Is there some kind of rational explanation for this to have happened?"

Lucas stood and held his hand out as he stared at him. "Give me your hand."

Conner stood and held his hand out. Shivers ran down his spine as Lucas took it and closed his eyes.

They stood in silence for several long minutes before Lucas opened his eyes and dropped Conner's hand. He sat and didn't take his gaze off the other man.

"I know what happened. Are you sure you want to me to tell you?"

"I'm sure. Just tell me," Conner said with a weary sigh.

"I don't think you'll like what I'm about to say," Lucas said.

Conner nodded and gave him a small smile. "I understand. Make it quick so it will hurt less. Like, when you pull off a bandage."

"Here goes." Lucas took a deep breath. "From what I could sense, you've got some kind of nature magic to allow you to breathe life back to plants."

Conner snorted and sat back, before he draped his arms over the arms of the chair. "You were right. I didn't want to know."

Lucas grinned. "That's about all I can tell you right now. You may have to do some research into your lineage."

"Great," Conner said. "I knew my brother should've come with me." He shook Lucas' hand and took back the sprig. "Not what I wanted to hear, but thanks for telling me anyway."

"Who are your parents?"

"Miss Dee asked me the same thing. My father, Silas Andrews, passed away a couple of years ago, and my mother is Katherine Andrews." Conner stared at him. "Why is who my parents are so important? What don't you and Miss Dee want to tell me?"

"Silas Andrews," Lucas said as his phone rang again. "I never thought I'd hear his name again. As for why we need to know your parents, you'll have to figure it out for yourself. However, come see me if you any other questions. I'll tell you as much as I can."

Conner walked back out to his car and stared at the mistletoe he held. "So, you and your kind keep Garland Falls on an even keel, right?" The sprig wiggled. "I didn't need this complication, you know." The sprig rolled back and forth on his palm and gave him the distinct impression it laughed at him.

"I don't know why this started now, but it needs to stop," he muttered.

He started the car and drove into town. He decided not to tackle the problem yet, and instead ignored it for now. He checked the time on his phone and saw he still had a little over an hour before meeting Mel. Now was the perfect opportunity to walk through the different shops. He wanted to get the owners' take about increasing tourism for the town.

Fat snowflakes floated down, and he stuffed his hands in his pockets. He should've brought his gloves. And now he'd been caught unprepared. He was happy to blame Mel for the distraction, since she had turned out to be such a nice distraction. He stopped at the first store he came to.

"Mac's General Store," he murmured. "This looks like a good place to start." He walked inside and a large man knelt on the floor to stock shelves.

"Hi," Conner said. "Are you Mac?"

"Yep." Mac stood up and dusted his hands off on his pants. He shook Conner's hand. "You must be the fellow Dee Warner wrote to. I've waited for you to stop by."

"Yes, I am. Word does travel fast in small towns,

doesn't it." Conner looked around the store. "You have a nice variety of merchandise here." He sniffed. "Do I smell popcorn?"

Mac nodded. "The smell of butter and salt kind of gives the place a comfortable vibe. Like when you're at home on a cold, winter's night."

He had to agree. The popcorn made him think of when he and his dad and brother would go to the movies. His mother never liked the types of movies they enjoyed. As he walked down some of the aisles, the hardwood floor creaked under his feet.

If Mac could fill a space, it looked like he did. Not one empty spot could be seen. In the middle of the store stood a rectangular candy counter with the popcorn machine centered behind it. There were household items, clothing, a few grocery items, and gardening supplies. Steps in the far corner led to the lower level where the toys were displayed.

"This is a nice store. You have lots of variety here." Conner looked around. "Did you ever consider you might expand?"

"Never crossed my mind. This is the perfect location for me. Everyone in town knows where everything is. Guaranteed if I don't have an item, Lou at the hardware store does."

Conner picked up a few items. "Do you worry any of the big box stores will open here and take your business?"

"Nope. We're too far off the beaten path for one of those places. The town wouldn't put up with one of those stores anyway. People like Garland Falls the way it is." Mac turned back to adjust some jars on the shelf. "Have you been all through Main Street yet?"

The myth of the town's permission to those it wanted rose again. "It's top of my list today. Garland Falls is a nice town." He paused. "Do you think if I could convince tourists to come here, it would hurt the small-town feel?"

"I think people will treat the town as nice as we do. If not, they won't be welcomed back."

Conner glanced at him. "The people won't welcome them back, or the town won't?"

"Maybe a little bit of both." Mac walked behind the register. "Let me get you rung up. There's plenty more to see on Main Street."

"I expect so." He shook hands with Mac. "Thanks for taking time to talk to me."

Conner left the store and headed into the bookstore next door. He talked to the owner for a minute, and the woman there was in favor of more tourists. So far, everyone told him they were in favor of him adding Garland Falls to his agency's website. Conner made notes in his notebook and continued on to the next place of business. The sign painted on the window read Renee's Creative Leather Goods.

He pushed the door open and saw a young woman at the back of the store, hunched over a worktable. The pungent aroma of leather and oil surrounded him as he made his way toward the back counter. On his way, he checked out the belts and gloves in the display counters, and bags on hooks along the far wall.

"Be with you in a minute," she called out.

"Take your time. I want to browse and see what you have."

After a few minutes, she walked up to him and shook his hand. "I'm Renee Callahan. What can I help you with? Do you need a special gift?"

"Callahan?" Conner said. "Are you related to Lucas Callahan?"

She chuckled. "In a way. I'm married to his brother, Parker. He's the groundskeeper at Warner's Bed and Breakfast."

"I have a room at the B and B. I know Miss Dee and her nieces, Mel and Alex. I haven't met Parker yet, though I have met Lucas."

"You won't see a lot of Parker until the snow clears. Not much work for a groundskeeper if he can't find the ground."

Conner smiled. "He doesn't shovel the snow?"

"In northern Minnesota?" she said. "Shoveling snow in Minnesota is like dusting in the desert. It's kind of pointless. Miss Dee gives him other jobs to do so he still has a paycheck."

"I saw him in the expense ledger Miss Dee showed me. She gives him a generous paycheck."

Renee moved back to her workstation. "Yes, she does, but he does a lot of work for her."

"I'm here to see if it would be beneficial to add Warner's and Garland Falls to my travel agency's website. What are your thoughts on increased tourism?"

"It would be good for the town. More people should come here. They'd like the peace and quiet. Garland Falls would be a great addition for your company." She bent over a piece of leather and hammered a stud into the end of it. "I'm not from here. I'm from back east. I came here to spread my grandmother's ashes and fell in love with the town."

"And one of the Callahans."

She grinned. "Yep."

Conner looked at a leather hair clip with mistletoe etched into it. "Can I buy this?"

"Sure. I guess this is the special gift for a special someone?"

He nodded. "Yes. I hope she likes it."

Renee wrapped it up as he ran his credit card. "I'm sure she will." She stopped him as he headed for the door. "Make sure you check out Heavenly Bites. Best cookies you'll ever eat."

He waved and walked outside. In the few minutes he'd been inside, snow had started to fall hard and fast. He saw what Renee meant about the uselessness to shovel snow. He checked the time, amazed how fast six thirty came around. As he hurried across the street, a small creature flitted by his face. He held his hand out and a tiny fairy with crystal wings landed on his hand. Before he realized what he saw, it flew off. Great. All this talk about magic had given him hallucinations.

He shook the snow off as he walked into the diner. Mel waved at him from the back booth they sat in the last time. He took his coat off and laid it on the seat.

"Did you accomplish what you needed to?" she asked.

"Somewhat, though I now have more questions than answers." He ordered hot tea and they both ordered the special again. "I did get to talk to some of the merchants on Main Street."

Mel sipped her tea. "What do you think?"

"I like them, and I think our clients will, too." He inhaled the scent of his meal and sighed when Sally sat their plates down. "I'd like you to tell me about the cookie shop. Everyone recommends them to me. What are your thoughts?"

Mel ate in silence for a few minutes. "I think they're one of the biggest selling points of Garland Falls. I think you need to do a whole write up on them."

"High praise." He finished his dinner and ordered them each a slice of lemon pie. "How's the tarantula problem?"

"Fred's decided to behave himself. He's stayed in his terrarium and hasn't caused any problems. I think you had an effect on him."

He sat back and wiped his mouth. "I'm not the spider whisperer, you know. I did what you did."

"Sure." She stood and put her coat on. "Let's head back to the carnival and see the progress."

"Even though it's snowing?"

"Especially because it's snowing."

Chapter Eleven

More booths had been finished, and the rest were close to completion. Conner found Callahan's setup right away. No one could miss the spread of bright red and white poinsettias if they tried. The Heavenly Bites booth had been finished, Christmas lights glowing against the sign. Renee waved as she put the final touches on her booth, right next to Bergetole's Pizza.

"Do you still plan to stay long enough to attend the winter carnival?" Mel said. "And maybe longer?"

"Yes, I am. I'm anxious to see the festivities. To get the full experience, I need to see the carnival for myself. It helps to have a first-hand account for the travel brochure." He held her hand. "And I'll stay as long as I need to. You know, to make sure I've gotten all the festivities right."

"That's nice to know." She waved to people she knew, then spoke again. "I've gotten some of the smaller repairs to the B and B done. The new furnace has been installed and so far, there haven't been any new disasters. I hope these problems won't make you change your mind about the listing."

"I don't think so. I still have time before I make my final decision." He smiled at her. "And I'll make sure to take a good long time."

"I'm happy to hear it." She tugged on her gloves. "I suppose we should head back. The later it gets, the colder it gets."

"You're right." He shuddered. "I can feel it through my coat."

She nudged him. "Florida guy can't take the cold, huh."

He nudged her back. "Nope. Us down south folks have thin skin when it comes to cold and snow. The cold doesn't affect you much, though." He winked. "I guess if you are a winter pixie, you'd be used to it."

"If I were a winter pixie, you'd be right."

They each drove their cars back to the B and B and parked in the small lot on the right side. As they climbed the short steps to the porch, Conner stared at the wilted sprigs of mistletoe hung over the windows.

"I'll come inside in a minute. I want to take in the view of the town from the porch." He stood for a moment before he spoke again. "It's very picturesque, isn't it?"

"Yes, it is. I'll wait for you inside." She opened the door. "Don't be too long. If you freeze, it could hurt our chances to be with your agency."

As soon as Mel had gone inside, Conner walked over to the closest bunch of mistletoe. "If anyone sees me talk to you, they'll think I've lost my mind, but here goes. I need you to bloom. Miss Dee needs you and whatever magic people think you possess."

He breathed on it, and the mistletoe's leaves opened wide as life filled it. The berries grew large before his eyes and new leaves sprouted. He stared at his hands, then cupped them around the plant. The stems lengthened a good two inches. Could Lucas be right? Could he have magic in him even though he didn't believe in it? If true, he'd have to question what he knew about himself. The juxtaposition of those thoughts would be he didn't believe in himself.

Time to go in. The cold had made him delirious. The temperature had dropped several degrees by the minute, and his head had started to pound. He'd go to bed and hoped he'd be back to normal when the sun rose. He might have to talk to Michael about this. His brother would be sure to point out he was crazy and if he didn't, his mother would.

He hung his coat up and found Mel and Miss Dee in the drawing room. "The cold has given me a bit of a headache. If you don't mind, I think I'll turn in for the night."

"Are you sure?" Dee said. "It's only eight o'clock, still considered early."

"I'm sure. Too much fresh air today. I think my sinuses are rebelling against the cold."

He went to his room and found a plate of brownies on the dresser. It looked like Alex decided to bake tonight. He bit into one, and marveled at the warm, rich fudge. How did she know he'd need some comfort food tonight? If he answered himself with the word magic, he would never talk to himself again.

****

"I think you found your hidden talent, Alex," Mel said as she licked the brownie crumbs off her fingers. "These are wonderful. You're one heck of a baker. Did you want to sell them at the carnival?"

"Since I decided to have a booth, I've started to put a list of baked goods together. Mrs. Hall said I can have a spot near Bergetole's Pizza and Renee's leather stand." She paused. "I left some for Conner in his room. My intuition told me he needed some type of comfort dessert tonight." She brought out the milk and two glasses. "I think your hidden talent is repair work."

"I believe you might be right." She propped her head up on her hand. "You have good instincts about people. Conner became out of sorts when we checked out the carnival progress. He went to bed with a headache." Mel reached for another brownie while Alex poured them both a glass of milk. "I think the town's magic makes him uncomfortable. He tries to deny it and the more he does, the more out of sorts he gets."

"If he doesn't want to believe in magic, maybe Garland Falls wouldn't be a good fit for him after all. Magic gets picky if it gets denied too long." Alex looked at her sister. "You'll miss him when he leaves, won't you?"

Mel turned her glass in a circle as she thought about the kiss they'd shared. "I will. I enjoy time with him, but he's not cut out for cold weather." She rolled her eyes. "And where do we come from? The winter kingdom. I don't think he'd do well when we have the annual family get together. He'd freeze to death."

"Mel, Alex, come here," Dee called from the foyer. "You have to see this."

The sisters hurried to where their aunt stood. She pointed to the mistletoe over the window to the left of the front door. The sprig had become bigger and healthier than they'd seen in weeks.

"What happened?" Mel said.

Dee turned to her with a huge smile. "I have my suspicions, and I have to say I like it. I hope whatever it is continues."

"Me, too, Aunt Dee," Mel said, as she wrapped her arms around Dee. "Me, too."

****

Conner laid an arm over his eyes while he held his phone to his ear. Of course, his mother would call as soon as the sun rose. Never mind the time difference. When Katherine Andrews wanted you, you talked to her. It didn't matter he hadn't even gotten out of bed yet. If he'd gotten more sleep, he'd be better able to deal with his mother. But thoughts of Mel had kept him up most of the night.

"I'm not done with my evaluations yet," he said. "I can't leave right now. The town has set up for a winter carnival. It could be a good selling point if we decide to list Garland Falls."

"Conner, you've been there for a week. I expect you to get back down to Coco Beach," his mother said. "Felicia has spent too much time with Michael. She's forgotten you."

He sat up and bit his lip to stop a retort which begged to come out. "Then maybe Michael is who she should marry, Mom. Does it even matter which one of us she marries? You forced the two of us together without any regard as to what we wanted. Felicia has always been more of Michael's type than mine. Felicia and I are good friends. You can't force us to have emotions which don't work for either one of us."

"After all the trouble I went through to introduce the two of you?" she shouted, making him wince. "The plans I made, the parties I've thrown for her parents, and this is how you thank me?"

"I'll be back as soon as I've completed my assessment of Garland Falls." He stood and walked to the window. "You'll have to be patient until I get home. Maybe you can sell me off to another one of your rich friend's daughters then."

He hung up and threw the phone on the bed. He loved his mother, but sometimes, she could be hard to live with and harder to listen to. What had turned her so callous to his and Michael's feelings? His father's death had hit them hard, but it had devastated his mother. Could she still be mired in grief for her husband? If so, how long could it go on? His father had been gone for almost two years. She should mellow out soon, shouldn't she?

He went into the bathroom and started the shower. He waited a few minutes, but the hot water never came up. Dread made his blood run cold when he knew he would have to tell Mel. She didn't need any more problems and he was about to give her a big one. He got dressed and went downstairs. He found Mel, Alex, and Dee in the dining room.

"Mel, I hate to tell you this, but there's no hot water," he said.

She sighed and laid her head back and closed her eyes. "Of course, there isn't. Looks like another trip to Lou's." She looked at Conner. "You want to come with me?"

"Sure," he said, glad to spend more time with her. "I can explore more of the town and check on the winter carnival."

She drove them down to Main Street and parked in front of the hardware store. She went inside and Conner stood on the sidewalk then headed into Heavenly Bites. He opened the door, and the scents of chocolate, vanilla, cinnamon, and coconut surrounded him. A slim woman stood behind the counter.

"Hi. What can I get for you?" she said.

"Nothing, thank you." Conner looked around and walked up to the case with four shelves of various kinds of cookies. "You have a lot of different cookies here. It's a nice selection."

"We try. My husband and I are always trying different recipes and, so far, we've had pretty good luck." She stuck her hand out. "Joanna Mines."

He shook it and noted the smudge of flour on her knuckles. "Conner Andrews."

"We've heard quite a bit about you," she said. "You're here to give Garland Falls the once over to see if we're good enough for your travel agency."

"Well, it's not the way I'd phrase it." Conner stared in the case. "Andrews Travel has a very specific type of clientele. I have to see if our clients would like to come here."

"And what do you think of our little town so far?" she said, as a bright twinkle lit her eyes.

He couldn't help but smile. "I think it's a wonderful place. The people are nice and, from what I've had so far, the food is wonderful."

She handed him a large chocolate chip cookie. "Try this and see if we measure up to your standards."

Conner took a bite and chewed slowly. This wasn't a cookie to be eaten in two bites. It needed time to be savored, to let the flavors swirl around before his stomach could enjoy the sweetness. "This is delicious. I've never had one like it in Coco Beach. You're a wonderful baker."

"Not me," she said with a quiet laugh. "The talent behind these treats is my better half. I only eat the cookies, not bake them. He's the best baker I've ever met." She leaned close. "Heck with marrying for money, I married him for his baking skills," she said in a loud whisper. "I'm his taste tester."

"I don't blame you. Let me get an assorted dozen. Whatever you think is best."

Joanna stared at him for a minute, then filled the box. "I think I've gauged you right. You'll find a great variety." She rang him up and handed him his change. "Come back any time your sweet tooth gets the better of you."

"Thanks, I will."

Conner walked down the street, the plastic bag in his hand with his sweet treasure inside. He would be sure to share these with Mel and her family. He got closer to Wilkerson's Garage and heard voices inside. He stopped and looked through the open bay door. A young man stood arguing with a shorter, stocky, older man, who threw his hands up in disgust and walked into the office.

"Don't you get cold with the door open so close to the end of December?" he asked.

The tall thin man, with long blond hair turned and grinned. "Nah. It gives me motivation to get my work done faster." He walked over. "You must be the travel agent guy. I'm Isaac Wilkerson."

"Once again, I have to marvel at how fast word travels in small towns." He shook Isaac's outstretched hand. "Conner Andrews. This has got to be the cleanest garage I've ever seen."

"I find it's easier to grab what I need if I keep my tools picked up."

Conner looked at the floor and the walls. At the back of the garage was a wooden, green door. It looked out of place, but hey, he'd seen stranger things in

Garland Falls. Like miraculous recovery of mistletoe and fairies with ice wings. "There's no grease or oil on the floor. The walls look like you painted within the past month, and I can't smell oil or rubber."

"Since the carnival starts this weekend, we want to have a nice place to show whatever tourists who come." Isaac closed his toolbox and turned to him. "It's been hard to keep the place neat lately. We've had more work than ever since the start of the month."

Conner sighed as he took out his notebook. Mistletoe magic again. "How much business does the winter carnival bring in? Do you get a lot of people who need repairs or help?"

"Sometimes, but this year, who knows? We'll go to the carnival and spread the word about our service here." Isaac placed some tools on the workbench while he considered Conner's question. "I don't know about the business statistics. We maybe do a lot? I'm not real sure. Mrs. Hall would be the one to ask about those kinds of stats."

"I've met Mrs. Hall. She's quite the dynamo, isn't she."

Isaac chuckled. "Yes, she is. Have you met any of the other shop owners?"

"I have. They're nice people." He held up the bag. "I met Joanna Mines at the cookie shop. I didn't get to talk to her husband, though."

Isaac turned back to the car with its hood open. "I expect he'd gone to his booth to put some final touches on it. Where you off to next?"

"I thought I'd walk through the carnival grounds and see what other vendors are there." He hesitated. "What do you think about what Dee Warner says? You know, about the mistletoe's magic fading and hurting the town?"

"If she says so, she's usually right."

Conner rolled his eyes. Another person who believed in magic. "Do you mean magic is the reason people come here for the carnival?"

Isaac leaned against the car. "I have to admit, ever since the mistletoe started to wilt, a lot of stuff has gone wrong. The work here at the garage has piled up since ours gave out last week. We need fresh sprigs or someone to rejuvenate the ones we have until the next batch arrives."

Conner tried hard to conceal his surprise at Isaac's words. He had started to rejuvenate the sprigs at the B and B, but not in town yet. "Okay, then. I'll let you get back to work."

How could he be the one person in town who had problems with the magical explanation? What about how the small sprig he'd gotten in the letter turned very healthy? And what about how he talked the bundle at Warner's to come back to life? There was the conversation he'd had with Fred, the tarantula, too. As of right now, he didn't want to hear one more word about magic.

Not even from himself, no matter how much sense the magical explanation made.

Chapter Twelve

"Lou, please tell me this is the wrong price. Water heaters can't cost this much." Mel said, as she wondered how to pay for this disaster. "Can they?"

Lou turned the catalogue around. "They can. I'm sorry, Mel. I didn't expect you to need one so soon after the furnace. I would've had one here already."

"I didn't either." She fought back tears. "How can we afford to pay for this? The savings account has seen much better days. This will kill us."

"I'll order it and we can talk about payments, okay? I can have it here tomorrow." Lou squeezed her hand. "It'll all work out, Mel. I promise."

"Thanks for the reassurance, but my hope has started to fade. With Conner Andrews here, it feels like everything wants to go wrong at once, so he won't list us with his company."

"I'm sure it's not the case." He already had the phone in his hand. "Go see Lucas. Maybe he has some news about the mistletoe."

She got in her car and drove out to Lucas' nursery. Good news would make her day so much better. She crossed her fingers as she held the steering wheel. Lucas needed to expand his parking lot. She squeezed into the last open spot and hurried inside.

Ray stood behind the counter, while Lucas helped Mrs. Hall and the other ladies on the event committee pick out several bouquets. Mel edged her way over to him and waited while they talked to him about their choices. When they left, she jumped in before someone else could get his attention.

"Lucas, I need to talk to you, if you have a minute," she said.

"Always have time for you, Mel." He escorted her to his office. "Today has been crazy. A lot of the vendors want flowers on their booths this year. They hope if Conner Andrews can post pictures of the carnival on his travel site, we'll attract more business."

"Good idea, but I need to ask you if you've heard anything, anything at all, about the mistletoe delivery?" She slumped down in the chair in front of his desk. "I need some kind of good news right about now."

He shook his head. "I'm sorry, Mel. It's like every batch has disappeared. I've got feelers out to everyone in every realm I know."

She sniffed back tears. "I don't know what to do anymore. The water heater went up at the B and B. Sometimes I think magic is the most finnicky element on the planet."

Lucas laughed and sat on the edge of his desk. "Don't give up hope yet. There may be someone here who can help."

"And you've decided to mention this now. Who is it?"

"Conner Andrews."

Mel jumped to her feet. "Are you crazy? He doesn't even believe in magic. How can he help?"

"Trust me. He can help. You have to help him believe in what he can do."

Mel folded her arms. "What can he do?"

Lucas raised his hands and backed away. "It's not my secret to tell. Check for signs around the B and B. You should notice some small changes."

Mel opened her mouth, then shut it. The mistletoe Aunt Dee showed her and Alex last night. It had been dying but then looked bright and healthy. "Conner can heal the mistletoe?"

"I didn't say that."

Mel scowled at him. "Sometimes, I don't know why I talk to you, Lucas Callahan."

He grinned. "You know magical beings, like myself and you too, can't say stuff outright. It's against our union contract."

"You are impossible. I hope your wife smacks you when she gets home."

Lucas laughed. "She will, if you tell her how little help I've been."

She turned on her heel and left his office. Why couldn't anybody be straight with her? If her aunt didn't need her help, she'd go right back to the winter kingdom and stay there until next spring. A small crystaling fairy flew around her face.

"Not a good time, unless you've got good news about the mistletoe," she said, as she waved the tiny creature away. "Besides, don't you have to gather the frost for the tree lighting this weekend? Shoo."

She got in her truck and sat there, even though she knew people waited for her spot. She couldn't delay any longer. She had to tell Aunt Dee about the water heater. She hoped Isaac's brother could come back out to help her install it. No time like the present to find out.

She drove to Wilkerson's Garage, and Isaac stood

out front as he waved goodbye to a customer. "Hey," she called as she got out of her car.

"Hey yourself, Mel. What can I do for you?"

"You won't believe this, but the water heater went up. Do you think Tristan could come back out to help me?"

He walked inside, Mel right behind him. "He won't mind. He said he hasn't had a lot to do and has picked up odd jobs to keep him occupied. Tell me when you need him, and I'll pass on the message."

"Thanks, Isaac. Lou says the new water heater should be here tomorrow. I'd better find Conner and get back to the B and B. I'm sure I'll have more problems to take care of when I get there."

"He headed toward the carnival." When she got in her car, he leaned on the roof. "Cheer up, Mel. Things can only go up from here."

"We can only hope."

She parked in the town hall parking lot and walked toward the sounds of laughter. The archway had been erected that announced the entrance to the carnival grounds. Crowds of people worked on their booths, hung decorations, or worked on the town Christmas tree. She loved the winter carnival more than any other of Garland Falls' festivals. As a winter pixie, she knew she had a stronger connection to this holiday, more than the others.

Children ran past her as they shrieked with laughter. Her mood began to lift, as it always did when she came here. She waved to people as she meandered along, looking for Conner. She admired how much work had been completed so far. She asked a few people if they knew where he went, and they pointed toward the end of the aisle of booths.

She walked to the back and didn't see him. She stepped farther into the picnic area and the trees around it. She stopped when she heard a quiet voice, Conner's voice, but who could he be talking to? She tried to make as little noise as possible, even though snow crunched under her boots.

She stopped behind a tree and spotted him. He cradled something small in his hands. Had one of the crystaling fairies been hurt? It couldn't be. She didn't see the telltale signs of frost on his gloves. So, who or what did he talk to?

She soon had her answer. He smiled and held up a dark green, healthy sprig of mistletoe. Her eyes opened wide. He denied a belief in magic, so what she saw shouldn't be possible. Should she ask him about it or not? He'd tell her if he could help their mistletoe problem, wouldn't he? But he'd said on multiple occasions he didn't believe in magic, and not mistletoe magic at all.

She backed up the way she came. If he wanted her to know, he'd tell her. If he'd fix more of the mistletoe around the B and B, she wouldn't have to repair broken appliances like furnaces and water heaters. She felt sure he'd tell her when he felt ready. It must be hard for him to admit he had more in common with the residents of Garland Falls than he'd realized.

She wandered through the carnival and saw Mrs. Hall in the midst of the setup. "Can I lend a hand?"

"I never turn down an offer to help," the stout lady said. "I think some extra hands are needed over by the entrance.

Mel hurried over and helped hang the direction

signs. One of the men called her to help steady the ladder by the Christmas tree so decorations could be placed near the top.

"Your booth looks great, Renee," she called when the other woman waved to her.

She helped the book stand finish their decorations and stood. She backed up to check her handiwork when Conner came up behind her. She turned to apologize and smiled when his arms went around her waist.

"You didn't have to wait long for me, did you?" he said as he held her.

"No. I knew you'd find me when you were ready." Internal shivers ran up and down her spine as goosebumps sprouted on her arms. Her heart raced and warmth spread through her as much now as the first time he held her in Dee's backyard. "Ready to go back to the B and B? The rest of the vendors will be here around sundown to finish their booths. Opening day of the carnival will be here before we know it."

"Let's go." He let her go until he held her hand, warming it in his own. "I wouldn't want to be in anyone's way." He stopped when she did as a group hurried by and into the town hall. "Who are they?"

"They're the Christmas choir. They perform at the opening ceremonies before the tree is lit."

He kept ahold of her hand as they walked back to her car. "Why don't you sing with them?"

"It's not a good idea." She grinned. "I sound like a dying walrus. Nobody needs to hear those noises at the carnival. What about you? Do you sing?"

"I used to, but then I got more involved in the family business and there weren't enough hours in the day. I had to give it up."

She squeezed his hand. "Maybe you can sing for me." Her cheeks heated when she realized what she said. "And Alex and Aunt Dee. We'll have our own little Christmas party."

He smiled and put his arm around her shoulders. "Sounds like a nice idea. Maybe I will."

Being held by Conner felt nice, like hot cocoa and warm cookies nice. If he would always hold her, she felt her heart would fly to the stars and stay there.

Chapter Thirteen

Conner sat back and laid his hand on his stomach. "Miss Dee, you've made another amazing meal."

"Well, thank you, Mr. Andrews," she said while she stacked the dirty dishes. "I'm glad you enjoyed it."

"I think your food has to be the number one point for the B and B." He stood and stretched. "I'll be right back." He went to his room and got the bag from Heavenly Bites. "I thought I'd get a treat for dessert tonight."

Alex lifted the box out and sighed. "You got us cookies from Heavenly Bites? Would you mind if I fall in love with you right now?"

They all laughed as he opened the box. Dee brought in four small plates and they each took one. Conner brushed the crumbs off his fingers. "After everyone told me how good their cookies are, I had to go in. I have to admit, I've never had cookies this delicious before."

"After Joanna and Davin got married, their quality went up even higher," Mel said.

"You mean these weren't always this good?" he said as he reached for another one.

"They were great before, but now they're out of this world." She finished her cookie and got up from the table. "If you all don't mind, I think I'll go to bed. I've got to help install the new hot water heater tomorrow. Isaac's brother is coming back early to give me a hand."

"I thought it would have to be replaced," Dee said. "I hope it's the last of the breaks."

Mel nodded. "Me too. If not, our bank account will break, and I can't fix money. We've got to get more people here. I can't think about this anymore tonight. I need to get some rest."

She walked up to the room she shared with Alex. On the second of January, they'd have to go home to the winter kingdom. She got ready for bed and crawled under the covers. She faced the wall and closed her eyes. If their luck didn't turn around soon, Dee would have to close the B and B. Conner wouldn't be able to list them if appliances continued to break.

She swiped at the few tears on her cheeks. Crying wouldn't help and would give her a sinus headache. As she started to drift off, she heard a voice. She eased herself out of bed and looked down at the porch. She couldn't see anyone, so she opened the window and leaned out. Conner's voice reached her, but who did he talk to? No one answered, so he had to be by himself. Why did he have to go outside to talk himself?

****

Conner waited until Dee had gone into her office and Alex went to the kitchen to wash the dinner dishes. He slipped out the front door and walked down to the next sprig of mistletoe and took it down. He cradled it in his hands and smiled. He could sense the little plant's life. The more he used this strange ability he didn't know he had until he came to Garland Falls, the less the itch in his brain bothered him.

"Okay, I'm sorry I called you a parasite plant, but

you are, you know." He waited a moment. "No, I'm not sure how I can speak to you or understand what you feel, but I know I somehow have the power to heal you. If I do, you have to use your weird magic to help the B and B."

He heard a small creak and looked around. He didn't see anyone and hoped no one had heard him talk to the small plant. "Look, I know I said I didn't believe in magic, but I have to admit, I've had some strange occurrences happen to me. I have this weird itch in my head, and it stops when I talk to you or Bobby's tarantula. I need you tell me how to get more mistletoe to Garland Falls."

The sprig in his hands bloomed and more berries formed along its stem. "You didn't tell me to go to the fairies, did you? I wouldn't know how to find them, even if I believed in them." He sighed. "Point taken. I can talk to plants and heal them, so why can't fairies exist."

He went to hang it back up and stopped as he listened to the small bundle. "I'm not sure what you mean. I'm more important to Garland Falls than I thought? How can I be the catalyst to strengthen the magic?" He waited another minute. "I thought a kiss under the mistletoe was only a cute holiday tradition. All right, all right. When the time is perfect, I'll know. Until then, have a good night." He hung the bundle back on the hook above the window. "I think I'll head to bed. If you can communicate with the others, tell them I'll talk to them tomorrow night."

He went inside and headed to his room. He muttered a good night to Dee when he passed her in the foyer. He hoped she hadn't heard him outside. He didn't need Mel and her aunt to think he had lost his mind. He promised he'd help, and help he would. Even if it meant he'd have to re-think all he knew about himself and magic.

****

"I heard you talking to someone last night outside," Mel said at breakfast. "Did you get a phone call?"

Conner coughed, then nodded. "I called my brother. He likes to be updated about the progress I've made here so far."

"Makes sense. You said he runs Andrews Travel with you?"

"Yes. My mother doesn't like the day-to-day business side of it. She's more of the social contact person. Her skills are parties and talking to the more well to do of Coco Beach."

Mel helped herself to more orange juice. "Parties are a lot more fun than business."

They both reached for the homemade bread at the same time. Conner smiled and held her hand for a moment before he let her go to pick up the butter. "I like the business side more. It's a real trial to be polite to a bunch of people you don't know and aren't sure if you'll ever see them again."

"I hope you don't feel that way about the people here in Garland Falls," she said.

"What I do is different from my mother," he said, as he loaded scrambled eggs onto his plate. "I'm here to meet people one on one. It's much easier than being crammed into a hall where everyone talks at once. I like the personal interaction."

"Good to hear." She got up as a truck pulled into the driveway. "Looks like the new water heater is here.

I'll catch up with you later."

Mel hurried outside and helped Tristan unload the unit. "Thanks again for coming out on such short notice, Tristan. I appreciate your help. And thanks for picking up the new water heater. I don't think Aunt Dee's little pickup truck could have handled it."

"No worries, Mel. Alex tells me you're quite the handyman around here. I think you might have some tinker blood in you." He paused. "Alex isn't here, is she?"

"She's in the kitchen. I think she's baking today." She grinned. "You want me to tell her you're here?"

"No, not if she's busy."

They wrestled the water heater down the stairs to the basement. Tristan got the old one unhooked and they moved it out of the way. They had it in place and Tristan checked all the connections and gave her a thumbs up.

Mel arched her back and groaned. "I didn't think water heater installation would take so long. Think it's ready to be tested?"

"One way to find out," he said. "Go upstairs and try it. It might take a few minutes to run hot, but it should work."

Mel ran up the steps to the kitchen and opened the hot water tap. She waited a few minutes, and sure enough, steam began to fill the sink as the water heated up. She hurried over to the cellar door. "We've got hot water. We do good work. Do you need help down there with the clean up?"

"No thanks, Mel," he yelled back. "I've got this."

Alex came in and patted Mel's shoulder. "We have hot water again? Awesome."

"Nothing a little tinker magic couldn't fix." She winked at Alex. "Tristan's downstairs. He asked about you. Since it's early afternoon, you should go talk to him. Maybe take him a sandwich or one of your awesome pastries."

"How nice of him to ask about me," Alex said, as her cheeks turned pink. "Do you think he'd like a cinnamon roll? Aunt Dee and I made some this morning."

"I'm sure he'd love it. Go ahead and take them down. I have to clean up. I want to let Conner know the hot water is good to go."

Alex wrapped a cinnamon roll in a napkin and headed for the cellar steps. "After you two are done, it will be my turn. I missed my shower this morning."

Mel went to Conner's room and knocked on the door. He opened it, his cell phone pressed to his ear, and waved her in. She stood by the doorway, and waited. A few minutes later, he hung up and turned to her.

"What's going on?" he said. "Any new disasters?"

"Bite your tongue. I wanted to tell you the new hot water heater is in place so you should be able to shower now. Sorry it took longer than anticipated."

"I wasn't worried. I knew you and Tristan would get it to work." He plugged in his cell phone. "Mrs. Hall called me. She wants me to come to town hall when I have a few minutes. Your town elders want to have a meeting to determine the advantages of being with my company."

She rolled her eyes. "I should have warned you the elders would want to talk to you. Don't let them bully you. If Mrs. Hall is by your side, they won't have a chance to get a word in edgewise. She doesn't put up with their political nonsense. If she thinks your agency is a good idea, they'll have no choice but to agree with her."

"I'm glad she's on my side then. I wouldn't want to go against her."

Mel laughed. "No one wants to go against her. Do you want me to come with you?"

"If you wouldn't mind." He took her hands in his. "I'd like to have you by my side."

"I'll be happy to go with you." She backed toward the door and hit the wall. "I'd better let you get ready. I should make myself more presentable, too. I'll see you downstairs."

She hurried to her room and showered and dressed in less than twenty minutes. He wanted her with him. She felt she could fly, even if she didn't have wings. Should she wear makeup? Should she put her hair up? How come she dithered about her appearance all of a sudden? Heck with the town elders, she wanted to look nice for Conner. Every time she'd been with him, he'd seen her in her work clothes or jeans. Time to look more presentable.

She got down to the foyer and didn't see him in the drawing room or the dining room. She decided to go into her aunt's office and take another look at the ledger. Maybe they missed some money somewhere. She stepped inside and saw Conner at the blue door, his hand placed flat against it.

"What are you doing in here?" she said.

"Miss Dee said I could take another look at the repair sheet and the finances while I waited for you." He stared at her. "Why is this door so cold? And please, tell me the truth."

"It leads outside to the back of the house."

He twisted the knob and she sucked in a sharp breath. "If I open this door, what will I see?"

"The B and B's backyard," she said, as tried to keep the tremors from her voice.

He let go of the doorknob and walked over to her. "If it's the backyard, why are you so afraid of me opening it?"

She turned around and walked back to the office door. "You'll be late for your meeting with the town elders. We should go."

If he'd opened the blue door, he'd get hit in the face with snow. The door led to the winter kingdom and her true home.

****

When Conner first entered Dee's office, he had every intention to go through the books again. He'd seen the list of repairs on top of the desk. Mel had checked off quite a number of small jobs, the furnace, and the water heater. She tried so hard to make the B and B perfect. He didn't realize when he'd arrived how much the town depended on him listing Garland Falls with his agency.

He'd stared at his hands. He also had other skills which could help the town. He paced in the small room as he didn't like the path his thoughts took. They had started down the road that led to magic. He sighed. It appeared he had some magic in him, whether he wanted to acknowledge it or not.

His pacing had taken him near a narrow, pale blue door. As he passed it, an icy blast of air chilled the back of his neck. He laid his hand on it and pulled it back as though he'd gotten shocked. Cold numbed his whole hand. He turned the knob and opened it a crack to peek through.

Snowflakes had swirled around his face. In the distance, a different landscape from the area around the B and B appeared. Bright lights sparkled in the distance, and he could swear he heard singing. What could be out there and who'd want to live in such an environment? He'd started to step through when he heard footsteps in the foyer.

When Mel caught him there, he had asked her straight out. She said it led to the backyard, but he didn't believe her. If she'd told him the truth, he might have asked to go through to see the land beyond. She had acted afraid of telling him. Well, he'd had himself to blame. He'd scoffed at magic and fairies at every opportunity.

As she drove them to town hall, he glanced at her. "Mel, what's behind the door in your aunt's office? Tell me the truth."

She stared straight ahead. "I told you. It leads outside."

"Yes, but outside where? I opened it a crack and it didn't look like the B and B's property."

She stayed silent until she parked. She shut the engine off and turned to him. "I can't tell you because you won't believe me. Can we drop the subject, please?"

He took her hand. "Mel, can I make a confession?"

"Okay."

He licked his lips. "I may have been a little hasty when I discounted magic."

"You can't be serious. What changed your mind?"

He opened the truck's door. "Let's say, I've had some strange things happen to me ever since I got here. Magic is the only explanation that makes sense."

She got out and walked over to him. "You'd better be careful. Before you know it, you'll believe in Santa, too."

"We'll see." He cupped her cheek and smiled. "Let's get inside."

Chapter Fourteen

Mel and Conner walked into Mayor Jacobs' office. The town elders were already there, seated to the right, their gazes everywhere but at the lady in front of the desk. Mrs. Hall stood there, her arms crossed, a stern look on her face.

"I told you he'd be here on time," Mrs. Hall said. "I swear, I have no idea why I continue to put up with you and all your ridiculous blustering."

Conner stepped forward. "Mayor Jacobs, I'm Conner Andrews. I'm glad you've taken time out of your busy schedule to meet with me."

The mayor turned a smug smile to Mrs. Hall. "You see, Adelaide? He has the proper manner to speak with a town leader."

She harrumphed. "Because he doesn't know you like I do."

The mayor gestured to the chairs in front of his desk. "Mr. Andrews, we wanted to have this face-to-face with you to judge what kind of man you are. We want to know if your offer to help is sincere or if you're here to ridicule us."

"I understand, mayor. I promise, I'm here to help." He pulled his cell phone out of his pocket, thankful the internet loaded. "I've pulled up my company's website. As you can see, we are A plus rated with the Better Business Bureau. Our clients have left testimonials as to our service. We take pride in listing the best places."

"And you think Garland Falls might be suitable for your clients?" The elders looked at each other and made disapproving noises. "We're a small town," the mayor continued. "We don't have fancy shops and restaurants. There's not a lot to do here."

Conner smiled when Mrs. Hall gave out a loud sigh behind him. "Mayor, I have to disagree with you. I've read over the list of events Mrs. Hall gave me. There is a lot to do here. Do you not want me to list Garland Falls? Because I have to tell you, small town charm is popular right now."

"Of course not. I want to look out for my constituents, nothing more."

"I get it, but I've seen a lot of good points. You have a wide variety of shops, and the merchants are friendly. The food is delicious, and the cookie shop has some good treats." Conner glanced at Mrs. Hall, then let his gaze linger on Mel. "I'm excited to attend the winter carnival. I believe listing Garland Falls would be beneficial for your town and my agency."

The mayor stood. "I'd like to see the listing before you post it on this website you've shown me. Is this condition acceptable?"

"Of course. I may need your input on whatever you think might help attract tourists." He smiled at the elders. "Any insight you all may have can help. I do have one request, though. If the town can get internet access, it would be beneficial for Garland Falls to have a website. Tristan Wilkerson wants to learn how to set one up. What do you think?"

"If it will help my town and the people who depend on me, then I'm all for it." He nodded at the elders. "I believe you'll have our full cooperation."

"Thank you, mayor. It's clear why you're so popular with your voters."

He shook hands with the mayor and each of the elders before he followed Mrs. Hall and Mel out of the office. When they got outside, Mrs. Hall laughed. "You know how to play the politicians, don't you?"

"It's not that much different when I deal with the social elite down in Florida," he said. "You have to know how to butter people up, so you get what you want. You have to make them believe it's their idea, too."

Mel squeezed his hand. "Showing them your website didn't hurt either."

"I breathed a sigh of relief when it loaded. I had a moment there when I didn't think it would," he said. "I hope we can get WiFi here. It would help grab travelers' attention."

"You two will come to the opening ceremony for the winter carnival tomorrow night, right?" Mrs. Hall asked.

Mel nodded. "We wouldn't miss it. My sister, Alex, has a booth this year. She's become quite the baker."

"I know. I helped her find a good spot. I believe Tristan Wilkerson helped her get it built in record time. They make such a cute couple." Mrs. Hall walked to her car and opened the door. "Let's see how the Heavenly Bites crew likes this news."

Mel laughed. "Joanna and Davin don't have to worry. She doesn't do cookies. Just bread and other pastries."

"Good to know," the older lady said before she got

in her car and drove away.

Mel drove them back to the B and B as the sun started to set. "Aunt Dee should have dinner ready. Are you hungry?"

"If it's Miss Dee's food, then yes, I am. Go on in." He stood by the car and gazed at the B and B. "I'll be there in a minute."

She frowned a little. "You've spent quite a bit of time out here in the cold lately. I thought you Florida guys couldn't take it."

"I've become acclimatized to the freezing temps. They're not so bad once you get used to them." He kissed her cheek. "I'll be in soon."

He waited until she walked inside, then approached the next sprig of mistletoe. He ran his hands over it and breathed on it. "Grow, little bunch. Miss Dee needs you. Yeah, yeah, yeah. I already apologized for the parasite remark. According to all the plant books out there, your kind are a parasitic plant. I'm not wrong you know."

He moved on to the next bunch and the next. Soon, all the sprigs glowed with health. He stood back and admired his work. His fingers curled into loose fists. He wished he knew what sparked this strange ability in him. He'd never been able to do anything like this in Florida, except for the few times he convinced some dogs to stop barking. Maybe magic did exist in Garland Falls, and in him, after all.

****

Mel helped her aunt set the table. "Do you think Conner might have magic in him?"

"What makes you ask?" Dee handed her the napkins. "I thought he didn't believe in magic."

"I did, too, but he spends a lot of time on the porch and talks to himself." Mel folded the napkins and put them by each plate. "And every morning, the mistletoe looks better."

"So, he could be the one healing the sprigs?" Dee continued to set the table, a small smile on her face. "I believe he wanted to be all about business and reality, not magic."

"So did I." Mel set three large potholders in the middle of the table. "You have to admit, things are stranger than normal since he got here." Mel stared at her aunt. "What do you know?"

"Nothing at all, dear." Dee walked around the table and hugged her niece. "What I do know is you like him, and maybe have a few stronger feelings, too. Therefore, you hope he's starting to believe in magic so you can show him who you are."

"Aunt Dee, you need to stop right now." She thought about him for a minute. "Just because he's tall, handsome, smart, kind... All right, so I do have a type and Conner is the type I have. Who knew?"

"I did. Trust me. He's the man for you," Dee said with a smile.

The front door opened, and the object of their discussion walked into the dining room. "I don't know what you made for dinner, but it smells great."

"It's beef stew and homemade bread. Sit down, Conner. Mel, call your sister down."

Mel sat instead. "Alex went out to dinner with Tristan. It's the three of us tonight."

Dee carried in the Dutch oven and placed it in the middle of the table. She spooned some stew into everyone's bowls while Mel sliced the bread.

"How did the meeting with the mayor go today?" Dee asked.

"Mrs. Hall went with us," Mel said, as she spread butter on a slice of Alex's sourdough bread. "Conner won over the town elders in no time. The mayor likes the idea of Andrews Travel listing Garland Falls as a tourist destination. He's even agreed to a town website, if we can get WiFi to work better here."

"Good news all around. I thought he'd be harder to convince."

Conner smiled. "Not with Mrs. Hall there. I could almost see her shoot daggers out of her eyes at him."

Dee laughed. "That's Adelaide, all right. She's kept the elders in line for years. What do you two plan to do tonight?"

Mel glanced out the window. "The way the snow is coming down, I thought Conner and I should stay in and see what else he wants to accomplish to make sure the B and B is perfect for Andrews Travel."

"Good idea. It's way too cold to be traipsing around in the dark." He drank some of the hot tea Dee poured for him. "Will this weather hurt those who have to finish their set up for the winter carnival?"

"Nope. There's not much left for them to do," Mel said. "If they can't finish tonight, they have time tomorrow before the carnival opens at noon."

"I guess the people here aren't bothered much by snow."

Dee and Mel laughed. "Not at all," Dee said. "Most of the townsfolk were born here. Some are transplanted from other cities, but they stay in spite of the weather."

After they ate, Mel started to help Dee clear the table. "Don't you worry about me," Dee said. "You two go and work on how to make Warner's Bed and Breakfast appeal to the masses."

Mel led Conner back to Dee's office. She turned on the lights and grabbed the ledgers. She needed to show the progress she'd made with repairs and touchups to the Victorian B and B. When she opened the financial ledger, she groaned.

"What's wrong?" Conner said.

"We're about two dollars and fifty cents away from being in the red." She sat back. "Even with Lou not charging us right away for the new furnace and water heater, I've had to buy different items to make this place what you expected it to be."

Conner took the book and added the figures. He didn't want Mel to be right, but he couldn't deny the black and white figures. One more big repair and the B and B wouldn't have any money left. "Once Andrews Travel puts Warner's on our website with a high recommendation from myself, you'll have more money than you know what to do with."

"Are you serious?" Mel's mouth hung open for a moment. "I thought you said you weren't sure if we'd be a good fit."

"Those thoughts were before I spent time with you," he said, then quickly added, "And your aunt and sister. I've gotten to know the people in the town. Everyone made time out of their schedules to talk to me. A lot of businesses don't take time to get to know their customers these days." He stood and walked around the room. "I think Garland Falls is what my clients need in their lives."

Mel jumped up and threw her arms around his neck. "Conner, I'm so happy to hear this. Aunt Dee will be happy, too," she added.

She stopped and stared at him. He smiled and lowered his head toward hers. His breath warmed her lips, and her eyes fluttered closed. His arms tightened around her waist as she held on to him, anchoring herself before the lightness in her heart carried her away. The door to the office opened and they jumped apart.

"Hey, Aunt Dee. Good news. Conner has decided to list Warner's and Garland Falls with Andrews Travel."

"Lovely." Dee winked. "It's nice to see you two get close."

"We're not… I mean, we weren't…"

Dee waved her hand. "Pish tosh. You don't have to explain anything to me, young lady. It's about time you found someone you like more than Bobby's tarantula."

Both of them blushed at Dee's words. "But, what about when I go home?" Mel said. "What will my mom say?"

"She'll be happy for you. Good night, children. I think I'll read for a little bit, then go to sleep."

They waited until Dee left the room. Conner turned Mel to him and smiled. "Should we try again?"

"I think we should."

He placed a gentle kiss on her lips. She melted against his chest, happy when his arms went around her waist and held her tight. Her fingers tangled in his hair, and she reveled in the softness.

"Your kiss was worth waiting for," he said. "Mel, you're a very special woman."

"You're pretty terrific yourself." She laid her head on his shoulder. "What do we do now?"

"Now, we get back to work." He led her to the small sofa and grabbed his laptop. "I've got to get Garland Falls listed, and the sooner the better. We want people here for the winter carnival."

She grinned. "You're very business minded, aren't you?"

He gazed at her. "Well, you are a nice distraction, but if we want to help your aunt and your town, we've got to get our attention back to the matter at hand."

"Agreed." She leaned closer to see the computer screen. "How do we start?"

He tapped the keyboard and started to write about the B and B. "Now we let this sit for a few minutes. I've got to have pictures to upload. Would you care to be in some of them? I've found if I have a picture of a representative of the establishment, it improves the ambiance of a place."

"Me?" She smoothed her hair. "Can I go make myself look a little nicer first?"

"Sure. I'll get some shots of the lobby and the dining room."

She ran up to her room to brush her hair and put on a nicer outfit. It wouldn't look right to have her picture online in such casual attire. The whole world would see her on the Andrews Travel website. Time to put on a professional appearance.

Chapter Fifteen

Conner took several pictures of the dining room and the foyer. He glanced up the steps before he stepped outside. He rubbed his arms, and wished he'd grabbed his coat. The snow fell fast and thick, but the overhang kept the porch clear. He continued his task of talking to the mistletoe sprigs and holding them to make their health return. A few more bunches to do, and the mistletoe around the B and B would be done.

He stepped back inside and warmed his hands up before Mel came back downstairs. He had her stop on the bottom step and took several shots with her hand on the decorative banister. He had her pose at the mahogany check-in counter and had her hold a coffee pot while she stood by the dining room table. Afterward, he took a couple of her by the Christmas tree in the drawing room.

"Tomorrow, I'd like to get a picture Garland Falls from the porch." He looked out the front window. "It's a great view and shows the town at the bottom of the hill. It should attract a lot of interest."

"Did you want pictures of the carnival?"

He nodded. "I'll get shots of the booths and show some of the people as they walk around. From what I've seen of the setup, it'll make an attractive addition. Do you think I could take a video when the Christmas tree is lit?"

"It shouldn't be a problem. You may want to double check with Mrs. Hall, though."

"She's supportive of any idea I have to do to help the town." He checked the pictures he had taken. "I'd also like to get the choir in there. Music always draws the crowds. If this works, you should get people here before Christmas."

She hugged him again. "Thank you so much for all your help. Aunt Dee will be so happy to hear this."

He held her close and reveled in the warmth of her body against his. "I'll do all I can to help you. You know something?" He smoothed her hair back when she looked up at him. "I could stay here all night and hold you."

"I feel the same way."

They walked hand in hand up the stairs. They kissed goodnight and went to their respective rooms. Conner crossed to the window and watched the snow as it swirled outside his window. He was happy Felicia and Michael had gotten together. He saw Mel as his future, and he'd decided he wouldn't go back to Florida. Cold and snow had grown on him in the past week. Garland Falls had themselves a new resident, even if it didn't know it yet.

He picked up the sprig of mistletoe and smiled. It had gotten healthier ever since he healed it. "I know," he told it. "Mel and I need to have a serious talk about magic. Of course, I believe you now. You don't have to sound so smug about it. I can admit when I'm wrong. Can you?"

He watched the snow fall a little longer. "You know," he said to the plant, "your brethren outside told me I'm important to help the magic get stronger. You have any thoughts on this?" He smiled. "I figured you'd agree. I need to know what to do, and I assume you'll let me know." When the sprig waved its leaves, he knew he had started to believe in magic.

Yes, he'd gotten work done on the B and B's listing tonight, but he'd done it with Mel. She fascinated him with her warmth, kindness, and humor. He'd never met anyone like her. As he remembered their kiss and how it made his blood race, he believed she had to be a magical pixie.

He laid the mistletoe on the bedside table and got ready for bed. He had a feeling a lady with blue eyes and honey-brown hair would invade his dreams. He couldn't wait to go to sleep and enjoy her invasion.

****

Mel ran a brush through her hair after she put on her nightshirt. She'd crawled under the covers right before Alex came in. She watched with amusement as her sister almost walked on air as she did her nighttime routine.

"I take it the date with Tristan went well?" Mel said.

Alex snuggled under the covers. "Who would have thought I'd fall in love with an elf from the tinker realm?"

"I've got news of my own."

Alex turned to Mel and propped her head up on her hand. "I hope it's good news. I can't take any more bad news."

"Conner decided to list the B and B with his agency. He's already taken some pictures and he'd like to video the tree lighting ceremony tomorrow night."

"I like to hear good news from you for a change."

She ran her hand over her comforter. "What else? Come on, I know you have something else you want to tell me."

"He kissed me tonight for the second time."

Alex leaned forward. "And?"

Mel fell back on her pillow, a wide grin on her face. "And how can I describe the most wonderful thing that's ever happened to me? He's so perfect."

"Would you say he's your type?"

Mel glanced at her sister. "You know, I told Aunt Dee the same thing. My type happens to look like Conner Andrews."

"We'll have to tell Mom tomorrow," Alex said. "We've found our consorts and it's not anyone at court."

"She'll be happy for us, and if she is, so will Dad." Mel turned out the light. "Goodnight, Alex. Tomorrow will be a big day."

****

In her room, Dee wrote a letter to her sister in the winter kingdom. She wanted to let her know her daughters had found their consorts and neither man hailed from the winter court. Alex had found herself a tinker elf and Mel, well, she didn't know which kingdom Conner came from, but it couldn't be Florida.

She sealed the envelope and opened the window. Two crystaling fairies appeared and took the letter. She closed the window and got into bed. She'd noticed the mistletoe had gotten healthier and knew for a fact Conner had been responsible. Conner Andrews was quite a catch. Knowing Mel had found someone she could love with her whole heart made her own heart swell with happiness.

She shut off her bedside lamp. The winter carnival would open tomorrow. With Christmas right around the corner, she'd love to see her nieces betrothed by Christmas Eve. With as much time as they spent with their chosen consorts, the possibility looked more and more like it would happen.

Chapter Sixteen

Why didn't his family ever want him to sleep in, Conner thought as he reached for his phone.

"What is it this time, Michael?" he said, his voice thick with sleep. "I'm not even out of bed yet, so don't tell me anything you can't handle yourself."

"I tried to stop her, so don't be mad," he said in a quiet, rushed voice.

Conner sat up at the panicked tone in Michael's voice. "Couldn't stop who from doing what? It's too early for riddles."

"You'll find out when you come down to the lobby of the B and B." His brother paused. "And you'd better be quick."

Michael hung up and Conner stared at his now silent phone. Dread filled him, chilled his bones, and choked off his breath. He suspected what Michael told him or tried to tell him, but couldn't deny what he feared. He threw on the clothes he wore the day before and dragged a brush through his hair. He took a deep breath and descended the stairs. Michael stood at the check-in desk with Felicia and his mother, who looked down her nose at everything around her.

"Mom, why are you here?" he said.

"I didn't expect you to give me such a curt hello." Katherine stared into the different rooms, as a frowned creased her perfectly trimmed brows. "I thought you said this place would be a good fit for our agency. I'm sorry, but I don't see any potential here."

"Hi, Felicia," Conner said. "I'm sorry she dragged you up here."

Felicia walked over to give him a brief hug. "Michael kept me updated about what you've said about Garland Falls. When he and your mother decided to come here, I wanted to see the town for myself. I also saw some of the pictures you posted to the website. Garland Falls looks wonderful."

"I'll have more to add tonight." He glanced over at Michael, who shrugged. "You picked a good day to arrive. The winter carnival opens today. You'll be able to see the town and meet the people."

"I hope you didn't think I planned to stay here any longer than necessary," Katherine said. "I want to leave this snow-covered, one-horse town sooner rather than later."

Conner stood in front of her. "You're not giving Garland Falls a fair chance. You came all the way from Coco Beach. I want you to treat everyone here at Warner's with respect, as well as anyone else you meet. Do we understand each other?"

His mother stood there with her mouth open. "Did you tell *me* how to mind my manners? Have you gone out of your mind? I came here to get you, that's all. I have no desire to interact with anyone in Garland Falls, especially Delia Warner."

Mel came out of the office and stared at the group. "Hi. I'm Melissa Owens. How can I help you?"

Conner turned to her. "My family needs three rooms."

"Sure. Welcome to Warner's Bed and Breakfast."

She turned the guest book around. "If you'll please sign in, I'll get your room keys."

"And how much will this rustic inn cost us per night?" Katherine said.

Dee walked out and frowned. "Less than what you spent on your dress, Katherine," she said, her words chilling everyone in the lobby. "Give Mel your credit card. I can assure you our rates are reasonably priced. Even you couldn't complain about them."

Mel looked at her aunt and tried very hard not to show the shock rippling through her at Dee's rudeness. Her hands trembled as she took the credit card. She handed a copy of the receipt back to Katherine along with her card. She placed the signed receipt in the cash drawer and handed them their keys.

Katherine looked her up and down. "Conner took your picture in the dining room. I saw it on our website. I must say, I wish he'd found a prettier model to showcase this place," she sneered. "Felicia Hawthorn is Conner's fiancée, and she would've been perfect to photograph. I suggest you keep your distance from him, young woman. I could tell from the look on your face you have designs on him. You can forget those notions. I plan to take him back to Florida to marry her."

Conner followed his mother up the stairs and entered her room right behind her. "You had no right to speak to Mel like you did. Felicia and I will not get married."

"You've defied me at every turn with this ridiculous trip. I will not be denied this marriage. All of my friends want their daughters to marry you."

He ran his hands through his hair. "You don't get it, do you? Felicia and I don't love each other the way you want us to. She and Michael have gotten close, but you're too blind to see it. They're the ones who belong together. Why can't you let us choose who we want to be with?"

Katherine threw her coat on the bed. "I suppose you want Plain Jane behind the counter downstairs. The only reason I can fathom is you want to hurt me."

He tried to hold his mother's hands, and she jerked away. "You know I'd never hurt you on purpose, Mom. Maybe I do want to be with her, and don't call her plain. Mel is a beautiful woman."

"Did you just tell me her name is Mel? No decent woman in her right mind would want to be called a name as vulgar as *Mel*."

"Her name is Melissa. She told you her full name when you checked in." Conner glared at his mother. "I don't want you to insult her while you're here. Her or anyone else in Garland Falls. Do you understand me?"

"I have no intention to move out of this room until we leave this town." She yanked open the door and pointed to the hallway. "Get out. Don't talk to me again until you come to your senses."

"Fine," he growled. "But we aren't done with this, Mom. Not by a long shot."

He stalked down to Michael's room and knocked on the door. When his brother opened the door, he pushed his way in.

"I knew you'd be here after you talked to Mom," Michael said. "How bad was the fight this time?"

Conner sat on the bed and scrubbed at his face. "Bad enough I don't want to return to Florida." He looked up and saw his brother grin at him. "You knew I'd decide to stay, didn't you?"

"Yep. I've always had good instincts. I got them from Dad."

Conner took a deep breath and let it out slip out a little at a time. "Michael, I have to ask you a question and please don't laugh or judge me, okay?"

His brother laid his hand over his heart. "You have my word. Tell me what's on your mind."

Conner held out the sprig of mistletoe, which had grown larger overnight. "Remember this little guy? This is the almost dead mistletoe Dee Warner sent to me in her letter."

Michael stared at it before he took it from Conner. "How did it come back? It looks healthy."

"Come with me."

Conner took him downstairs and grabbed his coat. He led him around to the other side of the house he hadn't gone to yet. He took down a bundle and held it.

"Watch this." He breathed on it and caressed the leaves. "I need you to come back. Miss Dee needs your magic more than ever."

As they watched, the leaves uncurled and turned a vibrant green. The white berries, which looked more like raisins, filled out to become bigger than they'd been before. The stems strengthened as new leaves sprouted and grew.

"Well?" Conner said.

Michael took the bundle and stared at it. "I thought Dad could do this, not you, and I never could. You got his magic?"

"Dad didn't have any magic. All the stories he told us about magic were stories. You two were the big believers, not me."

"He did have magic." Michael hung the bundle

back up. "Conner, the stories Dad told us, they weren't stories. They were all true tales from his childhood. He came from a mythical kingdom and passed his gifts onto us. Whether you want to believe it or not, we do have magic inside us."

"This is unreal." Conner ran his hands through his hair and paced at the end of the bed. "What about Mom? Does she have any gifts like this?"

Michael shook his head. "Dad never mentioned Mom was from another realm, like him."

They headed back inside and went into the drawing room. Conner sat in the wingback chair closest to the fire. "I need time to process this. All the years I denied magic, it turns out it's part of me and has always been there?"

"Yep." Michael stared at the fire for a minute before he looked at Conner. "You have a great talent. Think of all the good you can do. You heal plants. You talked the mistletoe back to life. You're like a plant resurrectionist."

"I know." Conner slumped in the chair. "But even when I heal the mistletoe, the magic here still feels off. I wish I knew how to fix it." He glanced at his brother. "The town kind of depends on it."

"I get it." Michael sat on the couch and leaned back. "So, tell me about Melissa Owens. She's a nice person and she's as pretty as you told me. She's the one, right?"

"Yes, she's the one. I told Mom, Felicia and I have no intention to get married. When she insulted Mel, I lost my temper."

"I heard the fight. I think your statement went over like a lead balloon."

Conner looked at his brother and nodded. "I'll be lucky if Mom ever speaks to me again."

"Speaking of which, did you pick up on the tension between Mom and Dee Warner?" he said. "I thought you said Mrs. Warner liked everyone."

"She does, or at least, I thought she did." Conner looked toward the doorway. "I'd like to know the history there. I bet it's interesting. I wonder what Mom did to her?"

"How do you know it's Mom's fault?" At Conner's scathing look, Michael held his hands up in surrender. "I retract the question."

****

Mel followed Dee back into the office. "Okay, you want to explain about the rudeness to Conner's mother?"

"What rudeness? I behaved with perfect politeness." Dee started to sort the papers on her desk. "I have three more rooms filled and the money will come in handy."

"Aunt Dee, I've never seen you be rude to anyone ever." Mel turned the office chair around so Dee had to face her. "Tell me about you and Katherine Andrews."

Dee folded her hands in her lap. "Silas Andrews was the best friend of Henry Warner, my husband. Henry and I were in love. Henry asked Silas to be his best man when we decided to get married. When Katherine and her family came to town for the winter carnival one year, Silas fell hard for her. I sensed the selfishness in her and tried to tell him not to see her."

Mel nodded. "You're good at picking up what people need or what they need to hear."

"Yes, but not what they *want* to hear. I told Silas

131

time and time again what I sensed in her, but the darn fool wouldn't listen. The more attention she paid to him, the more he refused to listen to me or Henry. He married her against the wishes of his family and friends. Katherine made him move to Florida to keep him away from here."

"Didn't he keep in touch with anyone?" Mel said. "I mean, a person doesn't stop talking to family."

Dee shook her head. "In this case, he did. Oh, he called a few times after he moved, but those became more and more infrequent, until one day, they stopped. We tried to call him, but we couldn't reach him. Then one day, out of the blue, Katherine calls me. She accused me of trying to break them up so Silas would leave her. Of course, I denied it, but she said he believed her. She had her hooks deep in him."

Mel pulled up a chair and sat and held her aunt's hands. "He built a successful business and had two wonderful sons."

"Those boys are the only good to come out of Silas's marriage. The sooner Katherine Andrews leaves my B and B, the happier I'll be." Her eyes narrowed as she looked up at the ceiling. "If she tries any mischief here, she'll soon find out I'm not a woman to be reckoned with. I'll call the blizzard trolls to dump four feet of snow on her overly made-up, pretentious head."

"Aunt Dee, don't you dare use your winter pixie powers like that. Mom would be very upset with you, and I think Dad would be too. He might recall you to the winter kingdom."

"You'll get no promises like that from me. I'll relax when she's gone."

Mel stood. "Why don't you go see Mrs. C.? She

might be able to help with your stress overload."

Dee patted her hand. "I think I will." She glared upward. "The less I'm around Katherine Andrews, the better I'll feel."

Mel walked back out to the dining room and noticed the mistletoe outside the window had grown bigger than the night before. She stared at it and jumped when someone came in the room behind her.

"I'm sorry. I didn't mean to startle you," Felicia said. "Conner said the winter carnival starts today. I wondered if I could get a ride into town with you."

Mel stared at Felicia Hawthorn. How could one woman be so gorgeous? She had long black hair and bright green eyes. She stood a couple of inches taller than Mel. Her outfit was perfect for the Minnesota weather, stylish, functional, and in impeccably good taste. Of course, Conner's fiancee would be perfect in every sense of the word.

"Sure," Mel said, forcing a smile out. "I'd be happy to take you. Wouldn't you rather drive down with Conner?"

Felicia laughed and Mel fought hard not to frown. She had a beautiful, light laugh. "Conner and Michael will talk for a little longer. When should we leave?"

"The carnival doesn't open officially until noon. We'll wait about here until an hour after it opens to give the vendors time to get to their booths."

"Great. I'll go get some rest. Let me know when you're ready to go." She stopped and turned back. "How will we get there?"

"Conner will drive us. His car has more room than my aunt's truck. I mean, you know, if they want to go with us." The longer Mel talked to Felicia, the more she found it harder and harder to be polite. "If not, we can take the truck."

"Whatever they want to do is fine with me." Of course, the black-haired beauty had a great smile.

Mel looked at the clock. "I'll let you know when I'm ready to go."

"I can't wait to get there." She winked at Mel. "The longer we're gone, the more time it'll give Katherine to cool off."

Mel watched her walk away and frowned. Why did Felicia have to be so nice? She already had Conner and looks any woman would want. And she agreed to spend the afternoon with her at the carnival. She laid her head back and groaned. Mel cursed herself for being a glutton for punishment.

She couldn't get enough mistletoe magic on the planet to help her fix this mess. Instead, she'd talk to Alex. Maybe her sister would have some good advice.

Chapter Seventeen

Mel ran up to the room she shared with Alex, grateful to find her sister getting ready for the day. She slumped down on the bed and buried her face in her hands, and let the tears fall.

"Hey, Mel. You want to tell me all about the shouting I heard earlier?" Alex turned and hurried over to Mel's side. "Oh, sis, what's happened?" she said as she put her arms around Mel and held her tight.

"Conner's family is here, and they brought his fiancee," she said in between hiccups. "I don't know what to do or say."

"He has a fiancee?" Alex's eyes opened wide at the news. "Why didn't he tell you he had a fiancee?"

"I don't know. He didn't act like a player. How could I have let myself fall for him?" Mel held onto her sister, as her shoulders shook while she cried. "And Aunt Dee doesn't like Conner's mother and caused a whole scene and now we'll lose the B and B."

"You fell for him because he's perfect for you. If he had already been taken, he would've been more interested in the business than you. I'm pretty sure his mother wanted to make you back off." Alex tried to soothe her sister as Mel cried harder. "I'm sure this won't affect Conner's decision about the B and B. Tell me about his fiancee. What's she like?"

"She's beautiful and nice and has a beautiful laugh.

Even her name is perfect. It's Felicia Hawthorn. I had to be dumb enough to say I'd take her to the carnival. Alex, what is wrong with me?"

"There is nothing wrong with you. You're a nice person." She smiled at Mel. "Conner has feelings for you, I know it. I've felt them get stronger every time he's near you."

Mel wiped her eyes. "You aren't saying that to make me feel better, are you? If you are, I'll be very mad at you for the rest of our lives."

"No, I'm not." Alex stood. "Get yourself cleaned up and let's go downstairs and make some lunch for everyone. After you get some food in you, you'll feel better." She made Mel look at her. "I made your favorite this morning, cherry turnovers."

"I love your cherry turnovers," Mel said. "Let me wash my face and blow my nose." She went to the bathroom and came out a moment later. "I look awful. Felicia is so much prettier than I am, especially now. How am I supposed to get through a whole afternoon with her?"

"Draw on the spirit of the holiday. Winter pixies can get through any crisis, personal or professional, during the Christmas season."

"You're right. I can do this." She took a deep breath. "I'm as ready as I'll ever be. Let's go downstairs and get this horrible day over with, sooner rather than later."

****

"I'm afraid Mom may have hurt Mel," Conner said. "She told her over and over Felicia and I were engaged. Both of us decided a long time ago we were friends and that's all."

"She told me that on numerous occasions." Michael folded his arms and leaned against the dresser. "We've had a lot of conversations while you've been gone. We've decided we want to get married."

"You know Mom will try to stop you." Conner walked over to stare out the window. "And she doesn't like Mel or Miss Dee."

"I don't know where she picked up all this hostility, but she'll drive everyone away from her if she doesn't get a handle on it." Michael joined him and stared at the snow which had fallen during the night. "It sure snows here a lot, doesn't it."

"I like that about Garland Falls. Even though it's plain snow, somehow, every time it falls, the town looks different." He glanced at his brother. "Mom has to know we'd never abandon her, as much as she makes us crazy with her control freak tendencies."

"I hope she does." He stared out the window. "You know, your magic could be opening up your senses to see the world in new ways." Michael gave him a side hug. "Dad would've been proud of you."

"Even if it took a long time for me to realize it?"

"Yep, even then. Then again, he knew you wouldn't be as open to magic as me. You have a lot of Mom in you." They stood silent, each with his own thoughts, before Michael spoke again. "Do you think you'll marry Mel?"

"If she'll have me after what Mom pulled in the lobby."

Michael walked over and sat on the bed. "She'll have you. I saw the way she looked at you. She had adoration written all over her face."

Conner smiled at his brother. "I hope you're right.

I've never felt like this about any other girl before. Mel is the one for me. I'm glad you and Felicia are together. I know you two will be happy."

****

Mel plastered a smile on her face when Conner and his family came down for lunch. "Felicia has asked to go to the carnival," she said. "Would you gents like to go with us, or do you have more work to do for the Andrews Travel website?"

Conner made a sandwich. "Since attendance at the carnival is work, we'd be happy to go with you two lovely ladies."

Felicia gave his hand a playful smack. "Oh, stop it, Conner. You know flattery doesn't work on us sophisticated women, right, Melissa?"

"Right," Mel said through clenched teeth and fake smile. "Dig in, everyone. Conner, do you think your mother would care for some lunch?"

The brothers looked at each other. "I don't think so," he said. "She's still upset, and we wouldn't want her to cause another scene."

"I'm sure Aunt Dee will make her lunch if she comes down while we're gone." She looked at the clock. "The carnival opened a few minutes ago. There's no rush, so we'll go in a little bit. The vendors still need to get set up and ready for business."

Felicia beamed her beautiful smile at everyone. "I can't wait to get there. Conner has told me about the booths and all the different items to buy and the wonderful food to eat. I haven't been this excited in ages."

Of course, she had perfect teeth when she smiled, Mel thought. *Why can't I not like this woman?* Oh, yeah. She had Conner, which made him off limits. Conner turned out to be reason enough to wish Felicia out of her life. When she went back to Florida, Conner would go with her, and Mel would never see him again.

She listened to the comfortable chatter while everyone filled up. Alex had put together a wonderful lunch with more homemade bread, lunch meat, salads, and fresh fruit. Did her sister have to go all out? Felicia complimented everything from the food, to the dinnerware, to the Christmas floral centerpiece.

Mel tried to not like her more and more. She took a deep breath and released it. She should be nicer to the woman. After all, she was important to Conner, so Felicia should be important to her, too. When everyone sat back to sip on their drinks, Mel put her napkin on the table.

"If everyone is finished, I'll help Alex clear the table." She stood and gathered the plates. "We can leave after we clean up."

Mel hurried into the kitchen and put the dirty plates in the sink. She had leaned on the counter when Alex came in, and let her tears fall. Her sister hurried over and held her tight.

"You're right," Alex whispered. "Felicia is perfect. In fact, she's a little too perfect. I think we're allowed to not like her on those principles alone."

"Oh, Alex, what can I do?" Mel said. "I've fallen in love with Conner, and he's promised to someone else. Someone much better than me." She sniffed hard. "I bet Felicia doesn't have to fix furnaces and water heaters and chase tarantulas."

"You never know," Alex said. "Maybe she's the queen of tarantulas and broken appliances."

Mel looked at her sister and laughed. "Thanks, Alex. You always know what to say to cheer me up."

"And you know how to make me talk to a guy I like."

Mel washed the dishes and handed them to Alex. "Speaking of a certain tinker elf, how are you and Tristan?"

Alex dried the dishes and stacked them in the cabinet. "We're good, better than good. He said he'd meet me at the carnival later. He went to help Isaac at the garage for a little bit. I've got to take my baked goods to my booth and get set up. Are you okay if I take Aunt Dee's truck?"

"Yes. I'll ride down with Conner and his crew." She sighed. "I wish Conner and I could be as free to be together as you and Tristan."

They finished the dishes and Mel stared at her sister. "Well, I can't delay any longer. Time to go out there and pretend to like Felicia. Pray I don't do something stupid, like tell her Conner is mine and she can't have him."

"You can do this. I'll be with you when I'm not at my booth. I'll be sure to help you not make any wrong comments."

Mel helped her sister pack the pastries she made into boxes. "Thanks. I'll miss you when you work at your booth. You have to make some money for the B and B." She grinned. "I expect you to sell out of all your products. Don't disappoint me."

"I wouldn't dream of it." Alex taped the boxes shut. "If I sell out, I'll have to do some serious baking to make sure I have enough for tomorrow."

"You were the one who decided to bake and now

your hidden talent isn't quite so hidden."

Alex laughed while they took the boxes out to the truck. "I'll take baking over repair work any day." She closed the passenger door and bounced the truck's keys once in her hand. "See you at the carnival. Make sure you stop by my booth. I'll be mad if you don't."

"You can count on it. Maybe I can convince Felicia to spend a lot of money there."

Alex crossed her fingers. "We can hope."

Chapter Eighteen

They arrived at the carnival and Mel asked them to wait while she helped Alex take the boxes. She cringed when Felicia said she'd be happy to help carry some, too. Then Conner and Michael pitched in and soon they had Alex set up and ready to go.

"Thanks for your help," she said. "This is Alex's first time selling and she's nervous."

Conner smiled at her. "We were glad to lend a hand. Alex will do great. Her pastries are fantastic. I'm sorry our mother refused to come. She might have been able to relax more."

"Her loss," Mel said. "Let's check out some of the stands. I'm sure Felicia would like to buy some Christmas gifts."

Felicia looked at all the booths. "I don't know where to start. I want to go to every booth right now."

"We need to stop by Alex's booth and buy some of her breads and pastries," Mel said. "She'll never forgive us if we don't."

Michael patted his stomach. "If she's got more sourdough bread, I think I'll buy all of it. I've never had anything so good."

Mel chuckled. "Make sure you tell her. She might give you a discount."

They started at the first booth on the right and made their way down the aisle. She glanced at Conner.

Would his fiancee try to push her out of the way so she could walk next to him? She hoped Felicia would be so enamored of the wares for sale, she'd never notice Mel had made her way to Conner's side. Why did he have to be taken, and by someone as wonderful as Felicia?

****

"I love the cold," Felicia said as they wandered through the carnival. She picked up a handful of snow and let it fall through her gloved fingers. "Florida's weather never changes, unless it's hurricane season."

Mel gave her a polite laugh. "Sounds dull. The seasons here change all year round. We had a spectacular fall last year."

Felicia sighed. "I'd love to see a real autumn. Palm trees don't change color as a rule. You're so lucky to live here."

"Yes, I am." She turned and waved to Conner and Michael. Each carried two cups. "Unless I miss my guess, they bought hot chocolate from Heavenly Bites. Best hot chocolate you'll ever have."

"I can't wait to try it." When the men arrived and handed them a cup, Felicia took a sip. "You're right, Melissa. This is the best hot chocolate ever."

"Call me Mel. Everyone does." Great. She'd given permission to Felicia to use her nickname. She had to have lost what little sense she had left. "Let's go try some of the games. Afterward, we'll get some dinner. We have a lot of time before the tree lighting ceremony. It won't begin until after the sun goes down."

They stopped to check out all the booths, and snack on different Christmas treats. Conner took her aside. "Can you show Felicia around? Michael and I need to take some more pictures, and I'd like to shoot an introduction video."

Mel forced a bright smile. "Sure. Not a problem."

She and Felicia wandered through the carnival and made sure to stop at Alex's booth. She watched Felicia buy several small items for Christmas presents. She murmured the appropriate responses when Felicia asked for her opinion. How could Felicia not know how much Mel didn't want to be here with her?

She clenched her teeth when Renee ran out from behind her booth to hug Felicia. The two laughed like old friends who hadn't seen each other in years. As it turned out, Felicia had been one of Renee's best customers at her online store. Mel nodded at the appropriate places when they recounted stories.

As they walked to a different booth, Felicia turned Mel to face her. "I think you have some resentment against me."

"No, I don't," Mel said, her defenses up. "I want to be professional. You know, project a good image for the B and B."

"I don't think that's the reason, but I believe I know what it is." She smiled when Mel remained silent. "Conner and I weren't ever engaged, and we don't plan to be."

"What? But Katherine said…"

"She said what she wants to happen, but Mel, it isn't what we want." She walked over to a bench and sat and waited until Mel sat beside her. "Michael's always been the one for me. Conner and I are only friends. We've been friends for years. The more our parents pushed us together, the more we knew we were meant for other people."

Mel stared at the ground. "I've been so unfair to

you. You see, Conner and I have gotten close. When Katherine said you were engaged, it almost killed me. I mean, you're so perfect and so much prettier than me."

"I thank you for the compliment, but I'm not as perfect as you'd like to believe. I've caused quite a few problems in my past." Felicia stretched her legs out and flexed her feet up and down. "Katherine Andrews is not a woman to be denied. What she says, goes. You should have heard the fight between her and Conner when we checked in."

"I had gone into my aunt's office to talk to her. Her door is pretty thick and not a lot of sound gets through. She's not a big fan of Katherine Andrews."

"I get it. Katherine is a hard woman to like." Felicia stood and shivered as the sun began to set. "Let's find the guys. I think I want to go somewhere warm to get an early dinner."

"Good idea. I'm getting hungry, too." Mel looked around the crowd and spied the guys. "There they are."

They found Conner and Michael at Lucas' booth. They looked in the middle of a serious discussion. The three men had their heads bent, and looked like conspirators as they planned a huge mission. After a few minutes, they stood back with huge smiles and shook hands.

"Mind if we interrupt?" Mel said. "Hey, Lucas. Do I even want to ask about the mistletoe shipment?"

"Hey, Mel, and no, you don't. I don't know what the problem is this year. I've never had delays like this before."

"Keep me posted." She turned to Conner and Michael. "Felicia and I are ready for somewhere inside. Shall we?"

****

Dee glared at Katherine when she entered the drawing room and sat near the fire. "Why are you here, Katherine? I told you to never set foot in Garland Falls again. You know what will happen if you try what you did last time."

"Delia, you haven't changed a bit," Katherine sneered. "You're still the same suspicious person you were when I first met you."

"I tried to be nice to you when you and your family first came to Garland Falls," Dee said. "I believed you when you acted kind to everyone. Then I found out what you said behind our backs." She leaned over her. "Behind *my* back. I decided you needed to leave my town. Now, you're the one person I'm suspicious of, and I still don't like you. I'm surprised Garland Falls allowed you back here."

"Your big problem is you didn't like how I told the truth about you to anyone who would listen." Katherine rose to her feet. "You were also jealous I took Silas away from you and Henry and this awful town."

Dee stepped forward. "You were wrong for him. You're selfish and self-absorbed and always have been. You married him because you could. Did you ever truly love him?"

"I loved him more than anyone on this planet," she shouted. "Silas was my life."

Dee watched Katherine sit and face the fire. "Then why did you keep him from us?" she said, her voice quiet. "If you loved him as much as you say you did, why would you let him break all connections with us, with Garland Falls?"

"I asked him to break off contact after I became

pregnant." She turned tear filled eyes to Dee. "Silas told me about his magic and what he could do. The magic I felt here scared me, and I didn't want my children to know about Garland Falls. So, I told him I never wanted them to come back here. I knew what would happen if they set one foot in this town." She wiped angry tears from her eyes. "And yet, you had to contact Conner. You wanted him here because you know what he is and what he can do, don't you?"

Dee took a moment, then said, "Yes. I know all about the magic he inherited. You were wrong to deny him his true heritage."

"And I'm sure you want to run right out and shout it to the world. Conner will come back with me, and he will marry Felicia."

Dee sat across from her in the other wingback chair. "Conner doesn't love Felicia, but anyone can see how much Michael adores her. Why do you want to push them together?"

"Because Conner is the one who deserves her."

Dee stared at her. "And what about Michael? He deserves his own happiness, too. Katherine, Conner has fallen in love with my niece, Melissa. I don't think you can break them up."

Katherine stood, and anger blazed in her eyes. "Of course, you think Conner would want your niece. I'll talk to him and make him realize what a mistake she is for him. She'll never have Conner."

Dee stared at the doorway long after Katherine had gone up to her room. She could wound more with words than any weapon she could use. She'd better not hurt Mel, Alex, Conner, Felicia, or Michael. She shook her head as she stared at the fire.

"Katherine, you haven't changed either," she murmured. She headed to the kitchen to start supper. Her nieces would be home soon. "You're still the most selfish, spiteful creature I've ever met. I'll be glad when you leave."

****

Conner drove them back to the B and B and they all got out, carrying small packages and some pastry containers. From the variety of bags they carried, they did most of their shopping in one afternoon.

"Will you come in soon?" Mel said. "Aunt Dee has supper ready, and I'm sure she still has some cinnamon rolls left." She turned to Felicia. "I don't think you've had a chance to try them yet. You'll love them."

"You two go ahead," Conner said. "Michael and I want to get some night shots of the town from here. I'd like to do some more commentary, too."

As soon as Mel and Felicia disappeared inside, Conner walked around the B and B, and talked to the mistletoe to heal it. Michael took pictures of the town while Conner continued his mistletoe task. As he finished the last bundle, the lights inside glowed brighter, and gave off a welcoming glow. They turned when a car crunched the snow and stopped in front of the B and B.

"Excuse me," an older gentleman called out when he rolled down his window. "We saw a sign saying this is Warner's Bed and Breakfast. Are we in the right place?"

"Yes, you are," Conner said. "How did you find it?"

"We checked out travel sites and this one popped up on Andrews Travel. We followed the directions and here we are."

The brothers walked over to the car. "Have you ever used Andrews Travel to book a vacation before?" Conner asked.

"No, the hotels and resorts they recommend were always out of our price range. This place sounded perfect for us. Do you know if they have any rooms left?"

Conner opened the man's door while Michael helped out his wife. "There's one way to find out. You came at the right time. The Garland Falls winter carnival opened today. The tree lighting is tonight along with a concert."

"Sounds wonderful," his wife said. "Do you work here?"

"No." Conner smiled as he shook the man's hand. "I represent Andrews Travel. I came here to add Warner's B and B and Garland Falls to our website. Can I help you with your suitcases?"

"Thank you, you're very kind."

They escorted the older couple inside. Conner found Mel in the dining room. "You'd better get to the counter. You have a couple who want to check in."

She stopped in mid bite. "Are you serious? How did they find us?"

"From the Andrews Travel website. Get a move on."

Mel hurried out and greeted the couple. She had them sign in and gave them a room key. Michael carried their bags to their room. Mel had an ear-to-ear grin on her face and a light in her eyes Conner hadn't seen before. Well, she did light up when they shared a kiss.

"They want to stay for the whole week. Conner, if we get more people, you and Michael may have to share a room." She ran around the counter and grabbed him in a tight hug. She gave him a quick kiss before she jumped back. "I've got to tell Aunt Dee."

Conner, Michael, and Felicia watched as she rushed around, trying to find Dee. As soon as she left the front, they heard another car pull up. Felicia walked behind the counter and Michael helped the new arrivals as Conner left to find Mel and Dee.

Mel, his Mel, had grabbed him and kissed him. A warmth spread out from his chest and stopped when it reached the top of his head and the tips of his toes. Michael grinned at him, and his cheeks warmed. He'd never been one for public displays of affection. He should have been embarrassed, but all he could think of was how right Mel felt in his arms.

Looked like the mistletoe still had a little magic left to share. He wished he knew how he could heal the sprigs. He greeted another couple as they walked in and shoved thoughts of magic to the back of his mind. Right now, he had business to attend to.

As he chatted with them, he thought about what the mistletoe had told him. If he kissed Mel under the mistletoe, as tradition dictated, would it be enough to strengthen the magic? If so, how strong would it be? Would he be able to revive Garland Falls? He smiled and knew he had one very wonderful way to find out.

Soon, more people began to arrive and, as thoughts of Mel crowded his mind, joy radiated out from him. This would be the best Christmas season ever.

Chapter Nineteen

Mel showed all their new guests how to get to the carnival before she and the others left for the tree lighting. Felicia's excitement bled over to her and the two danced around like children on Christmas Eve. When Alex came in to re-supply her booth, she dragged Mel into the kitchen.

"What's up?" She started to refill the boxes she'd brought in. "You and Felicia are best friends all of a sudden?"

Mel hugged her sister. "Felicia isn't engaged to Conner. She's in love with Michael."

"What about what their mother told you?" Alex said as she taped the lids closed.

Mel shrugged. "It looks like the guys want to go their own way, not their mother's."

"I'm very happy for you, Mel." She grabbed the boxes. "We'll talk more later. Right now, I've got to get back. I've had some great sales."

Mel walked out to the drawing room where Conner, Michael, and Felicia sat and chatted. "You'll love the tree lighting ceremony. It's my favorite part of the carnival."

"I can't wait," Felicia said. "Tree lightings in Florida are nice, but to see one with snow and the cold and cups of hot chocolate has got to be the best."

"This year will be great." Mel walked over and

took Felicia's hands. "This year, I have new friends to share it with."

She glanced at Conner. Of course, he might be responsible for the feelings which coursed through her. As she watched Michael and Felicia, she knew even a blind man couldn't miss the attraction between them. Her aunt had Katherine Andrews pegged. Her selfishness showed as she tried to force Conner and Felicia together.

They put on coats, hats, and gloves and drove back to the carnival. More people had arrived and milled around while they checked out the booths. Mel was happy to see Alex had a crowd around her booth. They got four hot chocolates from Joanna at Heavenly Bites. Mel stood on her toes and looked over the heads of the crowd.

"Come on," she said, as she grabbed Conner's hand, while Michael did the same with Felicia. "We have to hurry if we want to get a front row seat. Get your phone ready to take the video."

Mrs. Hall walked to the stage. She clapped her hands to get everyone's attention. When murmurs still floated on the breeze, she tapped the microphone and cleared her throat. Soon, the crowd quieted down.

"First, I'd like to welcome all of our new guests. We have a tradition here in Garland Falls," she said. "This town loves Christmas and all it entails. We work hard to keep the warmth all year round. After our choir sings some wonderful carols, we'll light the tree. The town tree stays lit until January second. The one year we turned it off, Santa couldn't find us, and no one got presents." She waited until the murmurs quieted down. "And now, Mayor Jacobs will speak for a few minutes." She glanced at him and frowned. "The fewer, the better if he knows what's good for him."

The mayor winked at her as he took the stage. "Thank you, Mrs. Hall. Our wonderful Adelaide Hall has said all there is to say. All that's left is for me to welcome one and all to our winter carnival and tree lighting ceremony. At this time, I'd like the choir to take the stage."

The green and red robed choir walked up to the stage and arranged themselves. They started with several religious carols before they broke into more traditional songs.

Conner leaned over and whispered in Mel's ear when the crowd joined in. "You were right about your singing voice, but I love it because it's yours."

"I told you," she whispered back as she smiled at him. "I sound like a dying walrus."

When the last notes died away, Mrs. Hall took the stage again. "Can we lower the lights please? Thank you. And now, it is with great pride, I light the town Christmas tree. The tree will stay lit until after New Year's Day. The lights on this tree will never fail. They light the way for Santa to find us, even on the darkest night. And now, I give you the Garland Falls Christmas tree."

Lights started at the top and turned on all the way down like a colorful waterfall. Snow began to fall, and the lights sparkled and danced with the flakes. The crowd exploded with loud applause, while some people whistled. Mel watched Conner pan down at the same pace as the lights. He'd taken video through the whole opening ceremony. She couldn't wait to see it on the Andrews Travel website. Conner would make the whole carnival look spectacular.

"Thank you, everyone, for coming. Please enjoy yourselves for a little longer tonight and be sure to come back tomorrow. We have lots of games, food, and wonderful items for sale." Mrs. Hall clapped her hands with the crowd and stepped down from the stage.

"I did worry for a moment," Mrs. Hall said to Mel. "I feared the tree wouldn't light."

"I think our luck has started to change." Mel pointed out the new guests. "We've had several new arrivals and they love the B and B. It's all thanks to new publicity from Andrews Travel."

"Did the new mistletoe arrive?" Mrs. Hall asked as hope lit her eyes.

"Not as far as I know, but good things have started to happen around the B and B. And we all know, when Warner's does well, it drifts down to the town." She glanced at Conner. "I think Garland Falls has a new good luck charm."

Mrs. Hall hugged her. "It does, indeed. You keep a tight hold of him."

"I plan to."

Mel and her small group wandered to the exit while most of the crowd headed for the booths. "What did you think of the opening ceremony?"

"It was so beautiful with the tree and the snow," Felicia said. "And the choir sounded wonderful. The frost made the tree look like it belonged in a fairy tale."

"I got the whole ceremony on video," Conner said. "Michael and I will go through it, clean it up a bit, maybe do some editing, and then we'll post it to the website."

"Now I'm kind of glad Mom dragged us up here,"

Michael chimed in. "I didn't know if I'd survive the temperatures, but after you've been out in it for a bit, you don't even notice the cold. You live in a magical town, Mel."

"I've been told so on a few occasions. How about we head to the diner and get some dinner. We'll have to hurry if we want a seat."

They beat the rush to the diner and ordered what they wanted. Mel smiled at each of them in turn. "I want to thank you all for your help this afternoon with the new arrivals."

"We were glad to lend a hand," Felicia said. "As a matter of fact, I felt right at home behind the counter. I'm a concierge at a four-star hotel in Coco Beach. I have to admit, I enjoyed the work in the B and B this afternoon. The smaller, intimate setting was a lot less stressful. The people were much nicer, too."

Conner picked at the edge of his napkin. "Mel, how would you feel if I stayed here?"

Her heart stutter-stepped in her chest. "I'd like for you to stay very much, but what brought about this decision?"

He looked at his brother. "Michael and I talked about it, and we think we'd like to open an office here. I'm sure some of the Garland Falls residents would like to travel, and we'd like to help."

"What a wonderful idea. Michael, would you move here, too?"

"If Felicia wants to come with me, I'd love to move here."

Felicia laughed. "You have to know I'd follow you anywhere. Mel, do you think I could work at the B and B? Would your aunt want my help?"

"I believe Aunt Dee would love to have you. I don't stay here all year round. My sister and I live in…somewhere else."

Conner took her hand. "If I stay here, would you stay with me?"

She squeezed his fingers. "You have to ask? Of course, I would. It's about time for me and Alex to be out on our own."

They finished the rest of their dinner and pushed through the crowd to go outside. They walked back to the town hall parking lot to get in the car. When they arrived at the B and B, Katherine stood on the porch, wrapped in her thick fur coat, while her foot tapped out a furious rhythm.

"It's about time you came back." She opened the door and pushed them all inside, except for Mel, who walked in behind the rest. "We're going home tonight. I've already packed your clothes. I won't stay in this awful town one more minute."

"What's happened, Mom?" Conner said.

She pointed at Dee, who had come out of her office. "Delia Warner has made my life miserable. I'm too afraid to eat whatever she puts in front of me. I wouldn't put it past her to try to poison me. We need to leave."

She turned on her heel, and Conner's voice stopped her. "You may as well unpack our clothes. Michael and I decided to stay in Garland Falls. We want to open an office here. We think it's a good business move."

Her back stiffened and she turned. "Oh, no you're not. I won't have you stay here and consort with people beneath us. I forbid you to go through with this foolish plan." She marched over and grabbed Conner's arm.

"You will come back to Coco Beach, and you will marry Felicia and make my dreams come true."

His eyes narrowed as jerked out of his mother's grasp. "Your dreams? What about what I want? You can't live my life for me, Mom. Michael and Felicia belong together, like I belong with Mel. She isn't beneath me, and neither is Miss Dee or the people of Garland Falls. If you want to leave, feel free, but the three of us will stay here."

Katherine straightened her silk business suit. "Then you stay without any help from me."

The brothers looked at each other. "Fine. You aren't on the business account, which means the agency money is ours."

Katherine's mouth dropped open. "You'd leave me alone and destitute?"

"Mom, you have more money in your personal account than we'll ever have in the business account, and that's a good chunk of change," Michael said. "And you aren't ever alone. You have tons of friends and all your social engagements. You won't even miss us too much."

"Of course, you know I'll miss you," she said, as her eyes filled with tears. "You're my children. I love you both, and I want you with me, but this idea of you staying here, it's ridiculous." She turned to Mel, her face becoming red with anger. "This is all your fault. You corrupted Conner with your foolish notions."

"Now wait a minute," Mel said, taking a step toward her. "Don't blame me if your sons want to get out from under your thumb. You've tried to control every aspect of their lives, and it won't work anymore. If you want to blame someone, look in a mirror."

Mel stomped toward Dee and the two of them left the group in the foyer. Dee led her into the small office and closed the door. "Aunt Dee, how can she be so nasty to everyone she meets? I don't understand how Katherine Andrews has any friends at all."

Dee wrapped her arms around Mel. "It's her way. It's a sure bet her friends are like her. She's had everything handed to her all her life, and it spoiled her soul. She may have a pretty face, but she's not very pretty on the inside. She's been selfish as long as I've known her. She came from money, and she's never had to go without. You can see it in her actions. She doesn't know how to be grateful for all she has been given."

Mel felt a tap on her foot and smiled. Fred had gotten out yet again. She picked the tarantula up and stroked his furry back. "I thought Conner told you to stay put after you and I had our own conversation."

The spider turned around and she got the impression he decided to ignore her. Dee left and returned a moment later with a small saucer of milk. She set it on the desk, Mel set Fred down, and Fred walked over to it and took a sip. He turned his many eyes to her, and she bowed her head.

"You're welcome, Fred." Dee sat in her office chair. "I could've slapped Katherine when she blamed you when Conner said he wanted to move here."

"Aunt Dee," Mel said, shocked. "Don't say that. Don't let her get to you anymore. She wants to ruin your mood so you'll upset the other guests."

Dee slumped in the chair. "With all the breakages around the B and B and feeling the magic fade in Garland Falls has me on edge. I can't find my good mood these days."

"My mood got better when Conner, Michael, and Felicia said they wanted to stay here." She hesitated. "If Conner stays, I won't go back to the winter kingdom."

Dee smiled. "You've chosen your consort, eh? I think Alex has, too. She and Tristan are almost glued together these days."

Mel cocked her head and listened. "I don't hear any voices out there. Do you think they're finished yelling at each other yet?"

"I'd say it's a safe bet." Dee rose to her feet. "I'd also bet Katherine still hasn't told Conner and Michael about the magic they carry in them."

Mel grabbed her aunt's hand before she could leave the room. "Conner doesn't believe in magic, and now you tell me he's got magic? How?"

"All I'll tell you is it came from his father. Silas lived in Garland Falls, and you know most of us are from different places in the fairy realms."

"What is Conner? Does he know?"

Dee patted Mel's hand. "I know what he is, and no, he doesn't know. Not yet anyway. I think you need to take him back to Lucas. He's the man with all the answers. I'm pretty sure he knew Conner's heritage the moment he met him."

"It would explain how the mistletoe started to bloom again." Mel rubbed her chin. "Is he one of Nature's fairies?"

"He's part of Nature, but I think you'll be surprised when you find out what his origin is. You'd better take Fred back upstairs. I'll stay in here until Katherine goes to bed. This evening has been a bit much for me, and I don't wish to talk or see her anymore tonight."

Mel sat and swiveled the desk chair back and forth.

She looked at Fred, who sat on the desk and watched them. "I suppose you know what Conner is too, don't you?" The tarantula stared at her. "Fine. Keep your secrets, but don't forget, I'm the one who finds you all the time. Come on, let's get you back in your home." She held her hand out and Fred climbed onto her palm. "Good night, Aunt Dee."

She left the office and Conner and his mother still argued, except now their voices had lowered. "Is everyone okay here?" Mel asked.

Katherine's eyes widened when she spied Fred sitting complacently on Mel's hand. She shrieked and the tarantula jumped up. Mel put her other hand over him. "It's okay, Fred. She didn't mean to scare you." She extended her arm. "This is Fred, my nephew's pet. He's harmless and he's pretty friendly."

"Oh, wow." Felicia hurried over and bent down to get a closer look at him. "He's so cute. Can I hold him?"

"Sure. Hold your hand out."

Fred walked over to Felicia's hand, and she giggled. "His hairy legs tickle. Hello, Fred. It's nice to meet you. My name is Felicia." She looked up at Mel while she stroked the tarantula. "He's so sweet."

"Fred is a very polite tarantula, but he's got to go back to his terrarium before he's missed. Come on, buddy. Time to go back to bed."

When Fred settled back on her palm, Mel smiled. "Good night, everyone. I think I'll turn in. I'll see you all in the morning."

Felicia followed her up the steps, still cooing over Fred.

Chapter Twenty

Conner fought to hold back his smile. His mother reacted to the tarantula as he and Michael expected. The horrified look on her face at the huge, hairy spider on Mel's hand had been priceless. The fact Felicia held the spider herself drove his mother crazy.

"What did you say about how Felicia and I don't belong here?" he said to Katherine. "I think we've proven we're a part of Garland Falls, whether you want us to be or not."

"I knew you never should have come here," Katherine said in a low voice. "As much as I loved your father, I told him this town would have a bad effect on you. Now, you've become like him. I tried to make you deny what you are, and I failed. You're leaving me for that *girl* who holds disgusting spiders."

Conner glared at his mother. "Mel is a gentle, kind woman and Fred is not disgusting. He's very polite, though he doesn't want to stay in his terrarium." He stepped closer to her and forced her to look up at him. "And I think you'd better explain how I'm like Dad. What haven't you told me all these years?"

Michael laid a hand on Conner's shoulder. "Maybe we should leave it until tomorrow. We're all tired and I think we'd better go to our rooms before someone says something they'll regret."

Conner glanced at his brother. "Always the

peacemaker, aren't you?"

"You've described me in a nutshell." He put his arm around his mother's shoulders. "Come on, Mom. I'll walk you up to your room. I know you're tired and frustrated and we did drop a huge bombshell on you tonight."

"Yes. I think I'll go to bed." She glared at Conner. "But don't expect me to apologize tomorrow. You can't make me change how I feel about this whole mess."

Conner watched Michael escort his mother up the steps. "She never did explain what she meant about me and my dad."

"Did you expect her to? You should've known she wouldn't tell you, Conner," Dee said behind him. "Go to bed. You'll feel better in the morning."

"I think I will. Good night, Miss Dee. You've been a real friend to me while I've been here."

Conner went into his room and sat on the bed. Well, this trip had taken a strange turn. Somehow, he couldn't be upset about the direction in which his life had taken. He walked over to the window and stared at the moonlight on the fresh snow. The light sparkled on the drifts and looked like stars had fallen to the ground. He smiled. He'd never been considered fanciful, but one week in Garland Falls had changed him.

Heck with going to bed right now. He walked downstairs and tried to keep quiet as he put on his coat. He walked outside and checked on the mistletoe. It had started to fade a little, so he imbued them with more health.

"I know this isn't the right solution," he whispered. "I realize I can't do it all for you. You may be healthy, but I can't replenish your magic. I know your time is over. As soon as the new bundles get here, you'll be able to go." He paused. "Yes, a kiss under your kin will happen between me and Mel. I wouldn't have it any other way."

Conner stared at the town below. Few lights were on. Everyone must have turned in for the night. Maybe tomorrow, he'd go see Lucas again. The florist had given him a few hints about his lineage, and now he felt ready for the truth.

He had a right to know about his father. His mother knew and had insinuated his father had magical abilities. Everyone had an idea of his lineage except him. Michael had even told him their dad had some kind of magic. He looked at his hands and wondered about the magic that let him deal with plants. Well, with mistletoe anyway.

He circled the B and B, and took a deep breath of the crisp, clean winter air. A thought struck him, and he walked to the back of the house. In the bright moonlight, he explored the rear wall. He found the window in Dee's office, but the wall was empty. Just as he suspected, he didn't see a pale blue door that led to the backyard. Mel told him, at first, she was a winter pixie, then made it a joke. Maybe she didn't kid with him after all.

He hurried back inside and hung his coat on the peg by the door. He slipped into Dee's office and made his way to the blue door in the corner near the window. He took a deep breath and reached for the knob. It turned as easily as before, and he opened it. Snow swirled around his face as he stared out into a land that wasn't Dee's backyard.

He closed the door and hurried back to grab his

coat. Whatever land it could be, he'd need a little more winter protection. He zipped up, yanked his knit hat over his ears, and went back to the door. He pulled it open and stepped through. Icy wind bit through his layers and chilled his skin. He looked back at the door once, then pushed through the deep snow as the wind howled around him as he walked toward a large building in the distance.

He walked closer then realized he'd headed straight toward a castle. It appeared to be made out of ice and snow. He ran his hand over a column by the doors and discovered polished granite under the snow. "This is beautiful," he murmured, his voice carried away by the wind.

The double doors opened, and two guards came out. "State your business, please."

"My name is Conner Andrews. I've got a room at Dee Warner's bed and breakfast." He pointed back the way he came. "She has this strange blue door in her office. It almost froze my hand and I wanted to see where it led." He looked up at the castle. "This isn't her backyard by a longshot, is it."

"No, it isn't. Come with us," the first guard said. "The king will answer all your questions."

Great, he thought. It's about time I got some answers. Wait. Did the guard say the king would answer his questions? How does one address a king? He took a deep breath. In a few minutes, he would find out.

The guards led him to a small drawing room where a couple were reading in comfortable chairs. "Your majesties, this man has come to us from Delia Warner."

"To be clear, she doesn't know I'm here," Conner

said.

The queen rose to greet him. "He's telling the truth, dear." She smiled and took his arm. "Have some refreshments brought in. Sit down, please."

When they were seated, the king lowered his glasses. "How is my sister-in-law? We've felt her recent agitation."

"I'm afraid my mother caused her to be upset. She and Miss Dee don't like each other very much."

A servant brought in a cart laden with different cakes and a pot of tea. The queen chuckled as she poured a cup and handed it to him. "It comes as no surprise to me. She's never liked Katherine Andrews ever since she married Dee's husband's best friend."

Conner paused, the cup halfway to his lips. "How do you know my parents? In fact, how do you know me?"

"I keep in touch with my sister on a regular basis," the queen said. "She keeps me updated on what happens at her home. I must say, it's nice to meet the man our daughter has chosen as a consort. You have our blessing."

"Your blessing?" Conner put the cup down before he dropped it. "Your daughter is Mel?"

"Of course. She didn't tell you she's a princess of the winter kingdom?"

"No." Conner's hands shook and not from the cold. "Well, she kind of told me. She said she's a winter pixie, but then made light of it, and she never mentioned she was a princess."

The king chuckled. "Our Melissa never tries to let it slip she's royalty. I never thought she'd marry a Drus, though."

"Hold up. What's a Drus?"

"You are, dear," the queen said as she refilled his cup. The king and queen looked at each other, and he gestured for her to take the lead. "A Drus is a nature fairy, a male dryad. Baby dryads have to come from somewhere, don't they?"

"Well, I guess, maybe, I mean yes, they do. So, I'm a dryad?"

"A Drus, dear. When you say dryad, it sounds like you're some skinny fairy woman, covered in leaves or flowers."

"Do some of my abilities include healing plants and talking to animals?"

The king guffawed. "Didn't Silas teach you about your heritage?" When Conner shook his head, the king sighed. "I suspect your mother had a hand in your lack of knowledge. What about your brother? Does he have any special talents?"

"He knows what people want or need to hear."

The king and queen nodded. "He's another type of Drus. Understanding is inherent in all types of dryads, male and female. You understand flora and fauna and your brother understands people. You two are very special."

"We are?"

The queen nodded. "Drus are very rare people. I can't believe your father was lucky enough to sire two. You and your brother will be revered in Nature's kingdom."

"Nature's kingdom," he murmured. "This will take some getting used to." Conner stood. "I suppose I should get back to the B and B. You've given me a lot to think about."

The king rang for the guards. "They will escort you back to the blue door and make sure you arrive with no problems. Please, come back and see us again."

"And let us know when the wedding will be," the queen added. "I'd hate to miss our daughter's marriage."

Conner grinned. "You may have two weddings. Alex spends a lot of time with Tristan Wilkerson."

"I'm not surprised she's taken up with a tinker elf," the king said. "She always did have a penchant for the unexpected. Thank you for the wonderful news."

Conner pulled his coat on. "Thank you for the answers, even if they're ones I'm having a little trouble with at the moment."

He followed the guards back to the door, glad for the escort. The way the wind blew the snow around, he'd be lost in a minute on his own. Soon, the blue door came into view. The guards waited until he opened it and stepped through. He brushed the snow off his coat and hung it back on the peg by the front door.

Up in his room, he walked over to the flower bouquet on the dresser and waved his hand over it. The blooms grew in size and became brighter. He walked back over to the mistletoe and picked it up.

"I didn't expect to be told I'm some guy dryad," he said. "I mean, a Drus. That does explain how I can talk to plants and Fred." He stared out the window. "Maybe I can help Lucas find the new mistletoe the town needs." The sprig wavered in his hand, and he knew he'd been correct to want to help. "Good night, mistletoe."

He got ready for bed and lay down, his hands behind his head. If he planned to make Garland Falls his home, he needed to help his town as soon as the sun came up.

How natural it felt to already consider Garland Falls his town.

Chapter Twenty-One

Conner found Mel, Michael, and Felicia in the dining room the next morning, as they helped themselves to breakfast. He looked around. "Where's Mom? Doesn't she need food to fuel another tirade?"

"She's gone," Michael said in between bites. "She left as soon as she could get a ride out of Garland Falls. She did say she's disappointed in our decision and will never come back here again."

Conner sat next to Mel and grabbed a cinnamon roll. "I'd like to say I'm surprised, but I can't. I think we hurt her more than we realized."

Mel handed him the basket of biscuits and spooned some scrambled eggs onto his plate. "I'm sorry. I shouldn't have come out with Fred in my hand. Almost every time you see me, I'm holding a large tarantula."

"Even taking Fred out of the equation, she wouldn't be happy unless she got her way."

They ate in silence and turned when they heard a car pull up. Mel got up and looked out the window. "We have more guests. I'll go get them checked in. If this keeps up, Alex and I may have to go home sooner than we planned. We'll need to make room for the extra guests."

She hurried out of the room and Conner stared at his plate. "Michael, I'd like you to go with me to Callahan's Floral Emporium today."

"Okay. Why? What do we need to get from a nursery?"

"Answers." He wiped his mouth and stood. "I found out some information last night you might be interested in. I think Lucas can dot the i's and cross the t's. You need to be there with me."

"Color me intrigued." He kissed Felicia's cheek. "What are your plans for today?"

"I thought I'd see if Miss Dee needed help around here." She stood and collected the dirty plates. "If I want to ask for a job, I'd better prove I can do it."

Conner and Michael walked out to his car. He brushed the snow off and headed into town. People were already out and about, with lines spilling out of Heavenly Bites and the diner. Shoppers walked in and out of stores. Conner waved to Renee as she set out a sign when they drove by.

They found a parking spot right in front of the floral shop. Conner found Ray at the refrigerator positioning new bouquets. "Can I bother Lucas for a minute?"

"Sure. He knew you'd be here today. He's in his office."

Conner and Michael made their way back to Lucas' office. He knocked on the door and opened it before Lucas called out to enter. "Sorry to bother you this early, Lucas, but I need to ask you some questions. This is my brother, Michael."

"Nice to meet you, Michael. I knew you'd both come for information." He leaned back in his chair and folded his hands. "Have a seat and I'll try to help you all I can."

Conner took a deep breath. "I went through the

blue door in Miss Dee's office last night."

Lucas gave them a smile. "And what did you think of the winter kingdom?"

"It's cold with too much wind."

"Yes, it is. Miss Dee's door connects to the kingdom of the winter pixies. The crystaling fairies come from there. They did a nice job with the town Christmas tree. They spread the right amount of frost."

"Yes, they did." Conner paused and glanced at Michael. "The queen told me Michael and I are Drus."

"Yes, you are."

Michael looked back and forth at them. "Well, it's nice to have a name for what we are. Dad never told us, and Mom ignored what we can do. She also forbade Dad to tell us about magic."

"I want to help get new mistletoe to Garland Falls," Conner said. "The bundles at the B and B told me their magic will continue to fade no matter how many times I heal them."

Lucas grinned. "This is quite a change from when you first got here. You told me you didn't believe in magic, remember?"

"I remember, but I'm not one to ignore signs when they hit me in the head." He leaned forward. "Michael and I want to move here. If Garland Falls will be our home, I want to help. What can I do?"

"Come with me." They followed Lucas out the back door to his private garden. "I'm also part of Nature's kingdom. I'm what's known as a Green Man. You and I have similar magic, but there are a few differences. I'm more of a protector of plants. You're their voice."

When they got to the middle of the garden, Conner

turned to Lucas. "What should I do now?"

"Listen. The plants always speak. You have to concentrate to hear them."

Conner stared at the plants and walked among them. He closed his eyes and cocked his head to listen to what the others couldn't hear. He ran his hands over the tops of the stems, and smiled when he heard musical voices in his mind. Their language couldn't be translated into English, but he could understand every word. Their language sounded different from Fred's. Still, what they said troubled him.

"The mistletoe doesn't want to be harvested," he said. "The sprigs don't feel appreciated. They've hidden themselves in a way they can't be found."

"What can we do to make the mistletoe want to come here to help us?" Lucas said.

Conner smiled and opened his eyes. "They want a prominent place on the town Christmas tree every year and they want to be on the city seal. If Garland Falls needs their magic, then they need to show the plant more respect."

"Let's go see the town elders." Lucas led the way inside and grabbed his keys. "I'll drive and we'd better snag Mrs. Hall on the way in. The elders won't say no with her on our side."

The hurried into town hall and caught Mrs. Hall on her way out. They explained what they needed to talk to the town elders about and she smiled. "Those old fools will love this." She patted Conner's cheek. "I knew you had magic in you. Come on, boys. We have a mission to accomplish. Then I have an event to oversee."

She pushed open the door to the mayor's office without knocking and stepped in, the three men right behind her. "These fellows and I have a few issues to talk to you about and I won't take no for an answer."

The mayor rubbed his eyes. "Must you make demands as soon as I'm in my office all the time, Adelaide?"

"Yes, because it's the one time I have your undivided attention."

She stood back and let Conner speak. "Mayor, I've found out what the delay is with the mistletoe." He waited while the mayor and town elders quieted down. "The mistletoe wants more respect from the people of Garland Falls. They want to be put on the town Christmas tree and to be added to the town's seal."

The mayor rose to his feet. "Do you mean a plant has dictated demands to us?"

Mrs. Hall leaned on his desk. "Would you rather be dictated to by me?"

Conner eased her off to one side when the mayor flinched. "More or less. If you give the mistletoe what it wants, it will allow its sprigs to be harvested and the town's magic won't fade. Do you agree to this?"

The mayor glanced over at Mrs. Hall. She'd folded her arms while Lucas and Michael grinned. "Yes. We'll make the changes right away. Tell the mistletoe to get here pronto."

"Thank you, Mayor Jacobs, on behalf of all the sprigs who will come to save your town."

Mrs. Hall went back to her office while the brothers followed Lucas out to his truck. Conner stopped him before he got in. "How do we let the mistletoe know what's happened?"

"When we get back, go out to the garden. Tell the plants. I don't know how it works, but word will get back to the mistletoe and we should have new sprigs by tomorrow."

Conner stared at his hands. "If I'd listened to my dad when he tried to tell me about magic and what it could do, I'd be more prepared for this."

"He knew it would take you some time before you believed," Michael said. "He wanted you to come to Garland Falls a long time ago, but Mom put her foot down."

"Thank you, Lucas." Conner shook his hand. "You've been a big help."

Lucas got in the truck. "Let's go. We've got a message to spread."

They got back to the flower shop and Conner went straight to the garden. He stood near the marble pedestal in the middle of the path and spread his arms out. The plants bowed to him and a slight breeze ruffled stems and leaves.

He turned to Lucas. "It's ready. The dryads will deliver all they can find tomorrow. The first priority is to get some of the sprigs on the Christmas tree, near the top if possible."

"You got it. What else do we need to do?"

Michael spoke up. "I have an idea. Why not make the new town seal design a contest? We could have people submit their ideas and choose the best one."

Conner grinned. "I'll ask Renee to design a prize for the winner. It will have to feature mistletoe, of course."

Lucas walked them out to their car. "I'll tell Mrs. Hall and she'll have the whole contest organized before you can blink."

"Great. We have a plan." Conner unlocked his car

and opened the door. "We'll get back to the B and B and let Miss Dee know what's going on. I'm sure she'll have a special idea, too."

Chapter Twenty-Two

"A contest to design the new town seal?" Mel said. "What a great idea. I think Garland Falls is lucky to have you two." She glanced at the counter where Felicia checked in new guests. "And Felicia, too. Aunt Dee loves her. She's a natural."

"I wish Mom would've stayed," Michael said. "I don't understand why she's so against magic. I mean, she had to know what Dad was and where he came from. Why did she marry him if she didn't like magic?"

"I don't think she'll ever tell us," Conner said. "We need to check out the town and see if we can find a good location for our travel business. Can you do without us for a little longer, Mel?"

"You guys go do what you need to. We'll be fine here, as long as Fred stays put."

As they hurried back outside, Mel watched from the drawing room window. It felt right for Conner and Michael to stay in Garland Falls. The town felt more complete, and so did her life. She'd felt it as soon as they announced their decision. The day had a brighter look, and they were the magnets which drew in new guests.

****

The week had flown by, and Mel, Alex, and Felicia had become inseparable friends. The sisters had absorbed Felicia into their family. Christmas Eve had arrived before they knew it. Anticipation for what the new town seal would look like had built since the contest's announcement.

"Hi, Alex," Mel said when her sister walked in from outside, her arms loaded with bags. She took some of the containers from Alex. "I can't believe it's Christmas Eve already. Is all good with you and Tristan?"

"Better than I could have ever hoped." Alex and Mel walked into the kitchen and set the grocery bags on the counter. "Do you think Mom and Dad will approve of him?"

Mel hugged her. "I think they'll love him. After all, he can fix whatever Dad breaks next time. For a king, he's not very graceful."

"When you're right, you're right. How about you and Conner? I'm glad you got your problems worked out with Felicia. She's nice and the guests love her."

Mel put the cold items in the refrigerator. "Felicia is all about Michael, which is perfect, because I'm all about Conner. Aunt Dee already wants her to stay and work here. She has a natural charm and warmth the guests gravitate to."

"She'll be a great addition." Alex closed the cabinet door. "If Tristan and I do get married, I want to move to the tinker realm."

Mel stared at her. "Will you be happy there? You're a winter pixie. You need the cold on occasion, and you know we need to be home around Christmas to replenish our magic for the year."

"I know. Tristan and I have talked about how to handle it when I have to go home. We'll have a doorway made so I can return to the winter kingdom when I need to."

Mel hugged her sister. "You've thought of everything, like always. Since Conner will live in Garland Falls, I'll stay here, too. I can get to the winter kingdom through the door in Aunt Dee's office."

Mel helped Alex finish packing up her new batch of breads and pastries. They walked back out to the check-in counter, where Felicia finished with new guests and handed them their room key. She smiled and waved at them before she picked up a cloth to clean the counter.

"She's too good to be true," Alex said, while she grabbed her coat.

Mel closed her eyes and concentrated. "She's got magic. I think she might be from the summer kingdom. It would explain why people are so drawn to her."

They walked over and Mel leaned on the counter and folded her arms. "Felicia, can I ask you a question and please don't think I'm crazy?"

"Sure. What do you want to know?"

She took a deep breath. "Are you from the summer kingdom?" she blurted out.

Felicia smiled and tucked her hair behind her pointed ears. "Busted."

"Aren't you cold here? Summer elves don't like the snow and cold temperatures."

"True, but my family considered me the black sheep of our clan." She shrugged. "I told you I used to cause problems at home. I wanted to explore other realms besides our home. They asked me to leave the summer kingdom, in a very polite way, and I did. I moved to Florida because it reminded me of my home."

Her eyes lit up as she looked around. "But then, I

came to Garland Falls and saw the snow. The cold invigorated me in a way I'd never felt before. I've loved every minute I've been here. To feel the crispness of a cold wind, to see the brightness of the winter stars." She sighed. "It's awakened something in me, something I didn't even know I missed."

She ran around the counter and caught up the sisters in a hug. "Then I met you two and Miss Dee, and Fred, and I knew I belonged here. Michael and I can start to plan our future." She looked at Mel. "Since you and Conner are a couple, Michael and I can be who we are and who we were meant to be. We can all celebrate Christmas together. I'm so excited to be with you."

"I guess Katherine didn't like you and Michael as a couple, huh," Mel said.

Felicia laughed. "You guessed it." She opened the door to Dee's office. "Miss Dee, do you mind if I go to the carnival with Mel and Alex?"

Dee came out and kissed her cheek. "You three go have a good time. I can handle things here. I've got to get lunch ready soon. Alex, I'll start the next batch of goods for your booth. You come back when you get hungry." She winked at them. "You know how the diner gets packed full during the carnival, especially since today is Christmas Eve. Now, go on and have fun."

The three women hurried out to Dee's truck and headed for the carnival. The guys would figure out where they went soon enough.

****

Conner and Michael found a perfect location and went to town hall to start the paperwork to get their business license. They'd have to call their old office in

179

Coco Beach. Their manager at the Florida location would be perfect to take over and they could always go back to help out if they needed to.

"All we need now is a place to live," Conner said.

Michael held up two fingers. "All we need is two places to live. I've lived with you long enough."

"Well, Christmas Eve has arrived," Conner said. "Do you think we should propose to our ladies tonight?"

"It should be a perfect night for it. The weatherman has called for clear skies." Michael said as they walked down the street. "Maybe we should buy rings for the occasion."

"Good idea," Conner said. "It's hard to get engaged without a ring."

They walked into the jewelry store and found themselves drawn to two separate cases. Each brother found the perfect ring for his special lady. They walked outside and high fived. This Christmas Eve would be the most exciting one they would ever experience.

****

Christmas Eve day had bright, blue skies without a trace of clouds. Snow gleamed in the sunlight. More and more people showed up to attend the winter carnival, thanks to all the hype the brothers had done on their website. Conner and Michael played tour guides as they took newcomers to different booths for food and crafts.

As the sun began to set, the mayor stepped up on the stage and called for everyone's attention. "I have the winning entry for the new town seal design contest. It depicts everything about the little plant which makes our town special."

He announced the name of the winner, and a little girl made her way to the stage. He handed her the leather wrist cuff Renee had made, along with a messenger bag with the new design. When the applause died down, he spoke again. "Thanks to the combined efforts of several prominent citizens, the new mistletoe has arrived. As you can see, we've placed it at the top of the tree so everyone can see it. Thank you to everyone for the effort you've put out for our community."

After his speech, the crowd went back to shopping, eating, and playing games. Conner and Michael walked Mel and Felicia behind the Christmas tree. They looked at each other and they knelt on one knee at the same time.

"Will you marry me?" they said together, while they pulled out the rings they'd purchased.

Mel and Felicia looked at each other, then cried, "Yes," at the same time.

Conner handed a sprig of mistletoe to Michael and each man held it over their heads. Mel and Felicia looked at each other and grinned. Mel stepped into Conner's arms and stood on her tiptoes and kissed him. Magic burst from them in a rainbow of color which flowed over the town. The same rainbow pulsed out from Michael and Felicia and mingled with Conner and Mel's. Plants that had started to wilt came back to life, brighter and more fragrant than before.

People applauded, as joy spread out from the couples and covered the entire carnival. Lights burned brighter and snow began to fall. Tiny crystaling fairies surrounded them and sent a cascade of light frost over them. They looked up and smiled.

"I think my parents approve," Mel said. "We've been blessed by the crystalings, and they don't do this for just anyone."

"I'm glad to hear it." Conner looked over at Michael who had also been covered with the frost. "You have any thoughts?"

Michael smiled at Felicia. "I think the winter, summer, and nature kingdoms are happy with us. How else can you explain the rainbows, the scent of roses, and all the flowers growing so fast?"

Conner laid his hand on Mel's cheek. "I think you're right." He glanced up at the mistletoe at the top of the Christmas tree. "Yes, you were right, too. If you want, I'll kiss Mel under you whenever you want me to. Deal?" He paused, then nodded. "This is a deal I'll be sure to keep."

"Is mistletoe your new business partner?" Mel said.

"You've discovered my silent partner." He wiggled the mistletoe over her head. "However, my new partner has deemed it productive to continue our activities."

"Merry Christmas, Conner Andrews," she said.

"Merry Christmas, Melissa Owens."

As she kissed him, he knew the magic of mistletoe had brought them together. The funny little parasitic plant had given them the best Christmas present ever.

They had all found love and received the gift of mistletoe magic.

A word about the author...

I grew up in Baltimore and graduated from high school in 1981 and married an Air Force man in 1982. We have two amazing boys who have grown into amazing young men. We spent sixteen years in New Jersey, four of them at McGuire AFB and the rest in south Jersey, right in between Atlantic City and Philadelphia. We currently live in the MidSouth, enjoying time with friends and dining on Bar-B-Que. Visit my website at www.annettemillerauthor.com

Thank you for purchasing
this publication of The Wild Rose Press, Inc.

For questions or more information
contact us at
info@thewildrosepress.com.

The Wild Rose Press, Inc.
www.thewildrosepress.com

www.ingramcontent.com/pod-product-compliance
Lightning Source LLC
Chambersburg PA
CBHW060106260626
47160CB00005B/1817